A Note from Stephanie about
a Double Disaster

It seems like I'm always getting into trouble, but this time I really topped myself! Becky gave me my first baby-sitting job, taking care of the twins. What a disaster! I can laugh about it now, but then . . .

Before I tell you what happened, maybe I should explain my family situation. If you already know the story, you can skip this part.

I come from a *very* large family.

Right now there are nine people and a dog living in our house—and for all I know, someone new could move in at any time. There's me, my big sister, D.J.; my little sister, Michelle; and my dad, Danny. But that's just the beginning.

Uncle Jesse came first. My dad asked him to come live with us when my mom died, to help take care of me and my sisters.

Back then, Uncle Jesse didn't know much about taking care of three little girls. He was more into rock 'n' roll. So Dad asked his old college buddy, Joey Gladstone, to help out. Joey didn't know anything about kids, either—but it sure was funny watching him learn!

Having Uncle Jesse and Joey around was like having three dads instead of one! But then something even better happened—Uncle Jesse fell in love. He married Becky Donaldson, Dad's co-host on his TV show, *Wake Up, San Francisco*. Aunt Becky's so nice—she's more like a big sister than an aunt.

Next, Uncle Jesse and Aunt Becky had twin baby boys. Their names are Nicky and Alex, and they are adorable!

I love being part of a big family. Still, things can get pretty crazy when you live in such a full house!

FULL HOUSE™: STEPHANIE novels

Phone Call from a Flamingo
The Boy-Oh-Boy Next Door
Twin Troubles

Available from MINSTREL Books

FULL HOUSE™ Stephanie

Twin Troubles

Mary Wright

A Parachute Press Book

A MINSTREL® BOOK

PUBLISHED BY POCKET BOOKS

New York   London   Toronto   Sydney   Tokyo   Singapore

This book is a work of fiction. Names, characters, places, and incidents are either products of the author's imagination or are used fictitiously. Any resemblance to actual events or locales or persons, living or dead, is entirely coincidental.

A MINSTREL PAPERBACK *ORIGINAL*

A Minstrel Book published by
POCKET BOOKS, a division of Simon & Schuster Inc.
1230 Avenue of the Americas, New York, NY 10020

A Parachute Press Book
Copyright © 1994 by Lorimar Television, Inc.

FULL HOUSE, characters, names, and all related indicia are trademarks of Lorimar Television © 1994.

All rights reserved, including the right to reproduce this book or portions thereof in any form whatsoever. For information address Pocket Books, 1230 Avenue of the Americas, New York, NY 10020

ISBN: 0-671-88290-2

First Minstrel Books printing February 1994

10 9 8 7 6 5 4 3 2 1

A MINSTREL BOOK and colophon are registered trademarks of Simon & Schuster Inc.

Printed in the U.S.A.

Twin Troubles

CHAPTER

1

◆ ◀ ◆ ◆

"Do you know who I think is totally cool?" Stephanie Tanner asked her two best friends.

Darcy Powell and Allie Taylor both said promptly, "Josh Hillman."

"You've only mentioned him about a billion times, Stephanie," Darcy added. "And that's just since school started this morning."

Stephanie giggled loudly. Then she shot a nervous glance over her shoulder at Mr. Mason, the school librarian.

The three girls had permission from their social studies teacher, Mr. Cole, to work in the library during their fourth-period study hall. They were supposed to be doing re-

1

search for their reports on customs of the Colonial era. Even though Stephanie and her friends were surrounded by huge piles of books, they weren't actually getting much work done.

"Josh *is* a hunk," Darcy said. "I love those ripped-up baggy jeans he wears." She smiled and ran a long, graceful hand over her dark curly hair.

Stephanie looked at Darcy and felt a pang of envy. *Darcy is lucky*, she thought. *When she smiles, she looks almost exactly like Whitney Houston!*

"I thought you had a thing for Brandon Fallow," Allie said to Stephanie. Allie tucked a piece of her long, wavy light brown hair behind her ear and grinned.

"He's definitely the cutest boy in the eighth grade," Stephanie said with a sigh.

"Well, what about that new boy?" Allie asked, her green eyes twinkling. "Ron something-or-other, who hangs out with Josh? Ron Martinez. Of course, I'm too scared to ever go up and say anything to him. But don't you think he's cute too?"

"Definitely," Stephanie agreed.

"I agree," Darcy said.

At that point in the conversation, Stephanie saw the librarian push back his chair and stand up. *Uh-oh*, she thought. She watched him walk soundlessly over to the table where the girls were sitting and loom behind Darcy's chair.

Stephanie made a face at Darcy, trying to warn her to be quiet. But her friend didn't notice.

"I don't think any of those guys is as cute as Caleb Parker," Darcy chattered on, oblivious. "With all that wavy hair and—"

"Umm . . . uhh . . ." Stephanie stammered, staring up at Mr. Mason. "Uh, yes, I definitely think so too, Allie. Caleb Parker, the creator of the cornmeal and lard bun, so popular in the Colonial era. I think we could all go for an inspiring American inventor like that."

Darcy stared at her as if she'd lost her mind. "Are you nuts, Steph? Caleb Parker is that boy on the soccer team with the great smile who—"

Behind her, Mr. Mason loudly cleared his

3

throat. Darcy jumped in surprise. Her eyes grew wide and her mouth dropped open.

Allie bravely tried to distract Mr. Mason with her sweetest smile. "Did you want to ask us something about our Colonial project, Mr. Mason?" she asked.

"Later perhaps, Allie. But right now I'd like to have a little talk with Stephanie over by my desk."

When Mr. Mason turned around, Stephanie made a worried face. *What have I done now?* she asked herself.

Darcy and Allie gave her sympathetic glances. "What do you think he wants?" Allie whispered.

Stephanie shrugged and pushed back her chair. "Who knows?" she muttered.

She slowly followed Mr. Mason over to his desk. Before he had a chance to say anything, she began talking really fast. "I'm sorry, Mr. Mason," she said. "About that overdue book. One of the twins got hold of it . . ."

Her voice trailed off when she noticed Mr. Mason looking blankly at her.

4

". . . Or maybe it was the dog, I don't know," Stephanie added weakly.

"Well, I hope you return the book soon," Mr. Mason said. "But what I wanted to discuss with you, Stephanie," he continued, "is the big fund-raiser we're planning to hold for the library in a few weeks."

"Fund-raiser?" Stephanie repeated hopefully. "You mean I'm not in trouble?"

Mr. Mason smiled at her and shook his head. "No, Stephanie. At least, not that I know of. You see, what with all the state budget cuts lately, the library has really been hard hit for money. We've had to cut our new book order list almost in half!"

Stephanie frowned. She loved taking books out of the library. She'd never even thought about where the money to buy the books came from. "If you can't buy books," she said, "how can you stay in business?"

"That's where you come in, Stephanie."

"Me?"

"You and the rest of the school. What we're planning is for each class to come up with an idea for its own library fund-raising project. The parents are planning an auction for the same day, so the whole school community will be involved."

"You mean you want us to have a bake sale?" Stephanie asked.

"Well, I suppose you could have a bake sale," Mr. Mason said. "As long as you don't make any of those Colonial cornmeal and lard buns you were talking about just now!" He shook his head and grimaced.

"Actually," he went on, "the teachers and staff are hoping you kids will really think big about your projects. Of course, we want you to have fun, but also to try to raise as much money as possible. We're hoping you'll get into that good old American spirit of competition. The grade that raises the most money will win a whole day off from school for a class picnic."

"Wow," Stephanie said. "That sounds totally cool!"

"You know, Stephanie," Mr. Mason continued, "I've been talking to your English teacher about you."

"Uh-oh." Stephanie made a little face. *Now what?* she wondered.

Mr. Mason smiled. "Mrs. Burns has nothing but good things to say about you, young lady. She raved about your winning essay for the Golden Gate Creative Writing Contest. In fact, because of your interest in books and writing, she thought you'd be the perfect person to head up the sixth grade's library project committee. What do you say?"

"I'd love it!" Stephanie answered happily. She was thrilled to know her English teacher had said such nice things about her. Mrs. Burns was her favorite teacher in the whole school.

"I knew we could count on you, Stephanie," Mr. Mason said. "Your committee can meet in here on Tuesday afternoons to plan your project. And remember—think big!"

"Think big," Stephanie repeated to herself as she ran back to her friends.

"Think big," she said again as she sat down at their table.

"Think big about what?" Darcy asked her.

"The sixth-grade project," Stephanie explained excitedly. "For the library fund-raiser. I'm the head of the project committee, and we have to come up with a really super idea for raising money for the library." Stephanie was frantically writing in her notebook as she spoke. "If we make more money than the seventh and eighth grades, we'll win a day off from school. And you know how the sixth grade and the eighth grade have always been rivals. It would be wonderful if we could beat those guys at something."

"Wow," Darcy said. "Anybody who could help win a day off from school would automatically become one of the most popular kids. Can I be on your committee?"

"Me too?" Allie added hopefully.

Stephanie laughed. "I already signed you up!" She pushed her notebook across the table and showed them what she'd written: "Library Project Committee Members: Stephanie, Allie, Darcy."

"So now all we have to do," Stephanie said, "is figure out who else to get to help us."

"What about Caleb Parker?" Darcy said eagerly. "I'm sure he can think big."

Stephanie shook her head. "Nice try, Darce," she said. "But the meetings are on Tuesday af-

8

ternoons. That's when the soccer team practices."

"Oh," Darcy said with a sigh. "So what about . . ."

"Excuse me. I couldn't help overhearing your conversation, and I just felt I *had* to tell you something."

Stephanie swiveled in her chair to see who was talking and found herself face-to-face with Jenni Morris, an eighth grader. Jenni was the head of a group of eighth graders who called themselves the Flamingoes. The girls in this snobby club wore something pink every day and had special bracelets and nail polish to show they were members. They thought they were the ultimate in cool. And for that matter, so did practically everybody else in the school.

As she looked at Jenni, Stephanie felt completely embarrassed about what she was wearing. Her new checked shirt, embroidered denim vest, and matching miniskirt had seemed totally cool when she'd put them on that morning. But suddenly, compared to Jenni's tight-fitting leggings and sweater, Stephanie's outfit seemed to her more like something a second grader might wear.

I'm giving these silly clothes to Michelle, she told herself, *as soon as I get home tonight!*

"I just thought you three might be interested in knowing," Jenni continued with a toss of her long brown hair, "exactly who is the head of the eighth-grade fund-raising project committee."

Stephanie sighed. "Somehow, Jenni," she said, "I think you're going to tell us—whether we're interested or not."

Stephanie, Darcy, and Allie were just about the only people in the school who didn't like Jenni and her friends. Earlier in the year, the girls had found out that the Flamingoes could tell lies and often be downright mean.

"I'm telling you for your own good," Jenni said. She stuck out her leg and admired one of her new, clunky platform shoes. *"I'm* the head of the eighth-grade project committee!"

She paused dramatically and waited for a response. After a long silence Stephanie said, "So, like, what are we supposed to do about it?"

"Never mind, Stephanie," Darcy broke in. "Let Jenni finish saying why she's so wild for us to know she's the head of the eighth-grade committee."

"I'm telling you," Jenni explained sweetly, "so you won't waste your time with your little planning meetings. You might as well give up now. The eighth-grade committee already has a totally hot idea. It's so neat, it's going to earn us at least ten times more money than the other classes. We'll definitely be the ones getting that day off from school! So you kids might as well not even bother."

Stephanie jumped up so fast her chair fell over and crashed onto the floor. "Oh, yeah?" she yelled. "Well, we'll just *see* who has the best project! You eighth graders think you're so great, but—"

Mr. Mason was on his feet, clearing his throat as if his life depended on it. "Ladies! Ladies!" he said, clapping his hands. "This is the library—a place of study. Please, *please* try to remember where you are!"

"Sorry, Mr. Mason." Jenni's voice was soft and innocent. "I was just helping these youngsters with their reports." She fluttered her fingertips at Stephanie, Darcy, and Allie. "I hope you understand what I was trying to explain, kiddies! Catch ya later!"

Mr. Mason sat back down at his desk. Stephanie put her hands on her hips and glared at her friends. "Do you believe her? How rude can you get?"

"Youngsters!" Darcy said indignantly. "Kiddies! Who does she think she is—our grandmother?"

"That girl is bad news!" Allie agreed. "But do you think she's telling the truth? Has the eighth grade already come up with such a great project that we don't even stand a chance? Should we really just go ahead and give up?"

"No way!" Stephanie snorted. "*I'm* not giving up! And you two aren't either. We're going to come up with the biggest and best project this school has ever seen. And why stop there? Let's make it the best project the city of San Francisco has ever seen. The best project the state of California has ever seen!"

"Why stop there?" Darcy laughed. "Why not make it the country? The world?"

"Okay!" Stephanie said triumphantly. "We hereby agree we won't quit until we come up with the best project the world has ever seen!" She set her chair back on its legs and plopped back down on it.

"Now," she said, "it's time to start thinking. What in the *world* are we going to do?"

CHAPTER

2

◆ ▼ ◆ ◆

That evening, Stephanie sprawled out on her bed, opened her notebook, and neatly wrote *Fund-raising Ideas* at the top of a blank sheet of paper. She felt as if she were starting something really exciting. If she did well on this project, she'd show the whole school how creative she could be.

"Let's see," she said out loud. She began making a list. "There's always a car wash. Or maybe a garage sale. Or we could sell candy bars door-to-door like the high school band did last year."

She gazed down at what she'd written. Then

she frowned and drew thick black lines over each item on her list. "Borrrrring," she said with a sigh. "Too totally unoriginal to be believed. I simply have to remember to think big."

The door opened and Stephanie's older sister, D.J., walked in. She was followed by her best friend, Kimmy Gibbler. Each girl was tightly clutching one of seven-year-old Michelle's hands.

"This, Michelle," D.J. was saying firmly, "*this* is your room. *Not* the room at the other end of the hall. That room is *my* room. Where Kimmy and I are trying to study. For our French midterm. Which counts for more than half our grade. *Comprenez-vous?*"

"Understanday voo-ay you?" Kimmy added.

Stephanie sat up and made a face at them. "Why did you two have to start studying a new language in the middle of high school, anyway?" she asked.

"Because my Spanish teacher said I was good at languages," D.J. explained.

"And because *my* Spanish teacher said I *wasn't* good!" Kimmy added.

"Well, Michelle can't stay in here," Stephanie said. "I'm trying to concentrate."

"You can't keep me out of here, Stephanie," Michelle pointed out. "This is my room too!"

"You can't argue with that logic, Steph," D.J. said with a smile. "Now, *au revoir!*"

"Tootle-oo-ay voo!" Kimmy said. The two older girls walked out of the room and closed the door behind them.

Stephanie made a face at their departing backs. "Okay, Michelle," she said, flopping down on her stomach. "You can stay in here. But you have to promise not to leave your side of the room. And you have to be absolutely, completely quiet."

"Okay," Michelle agreed. She wandered over to her side of the room, sat down on her bed, and picked up a large stuffed frog. Then, for what seemed like the millionth time that night, she started singing the new song she'd learned at school on Monday.

> *"One hundred giggling worms,*
> *Ho, ho, ho!*
> *One hundred wiggling worms,*

> *High and low!*
> *Oh, those wiggling, giggling worms,*
> *Watch them go!"*

After she'd sung the song once, Michelle jumped up and began singing it all over again. As she sang, she started going through a series of up-and-down wiggles and parading around the room.

Stephanie put down her pencil and glared at her. "Michelle," she said through her teeth, "I'm warning you. If you sing that stupid, irritating song again—just *once* more—I'll . . . I'll . . . well, I will *not* be held responsible for my actions!"

Michelle was so wrapped up in her song, she didn't hear a word. Instead, she wiggled and twisted right by Stephanie's bed and started the song all over again. "One hundred giggling worms, ho, ho, ho! One hundred wiggling worms, high and low!"

"That does it!" Stephanie announced. She leaped off her bed and started chasing Michelle around the room. Michelle raced away and let out a high-pitched, ear-shattering screech. At

17

that moment Becky opened the door and poked her head in. She was holding one struggling twin under each arm.

"Is everything all right, you two?" she asked. "I thought I just heard an alarm go off in here!"

"Everything *will* be all right," Stephanie said grimly, "just as soon as Michelle stops driving me crazy with that silly worm song!"

Becky laughed. "Actually, I think the worm song is pretty cute." She smiled down at the boys. "And Nicky and Alex love it. Right, guys?"

"Worms," Nicky sang. "Ho, ho!"

"Giggled," Alex sang. " 'N wiggled!"

"Oh, puh-*lease*," Stephanie groaned. "Don't get *them* started on that thing."

Becky laughed again. "Before I forget, Steph," she said, "I wanted to let you know I finally signed up for that film-editing course I told you about last week. So starting next Tuesday, I'll need you to come home right after school and baby-sit for these guys the way we said."

"Okay," Stephanie agreed happily. *Oh, boy!*

she thought. She remembered how excited she'd been when Becky had asked her to baby-sit. It would be like a real job—she'd have to be home every week at the time they agreed on.

"I can hardly wait to start—" she began. Then she stopped short. "Did you say *Tuesday* afternoon, Aunt Becky?"

Becky nodded. "Remember? You promised you'd watch the twins for me so I could take the class. That's why I went ahead and enrolled."

Stephanie moaned under her breath. Becky was absolutely right. She *had* agreed to baby-sit for Nicky and Alex every Tuesday afternoon. But that was before she'd known about the fund-raising committee meetings.

"Gosh, Becky," she said. "Is there any way you can switch to a class on a different day? I'm supposed to be running committee meetings at school on Tuesdays."

"I'm sorry but I can't, Stephanie," Becky said. She started to sound upset. "The course is offered on Tuesdays only, and this is the last time this particular teacher will be running it—and he's supposed to be the best there is. Also,

I've already put down a big deposit on it, which I couldn't get back if I dropped out. I was just so sure I could count on you for the baby-sitting.''

She came into the room and sat on Michelle's bed. Nicky and Alex immediately squirmed out of her arms and started throwing Michelle's stuffed animals onto the floor. "If you really can't watch the boys, Steph," Becky went on slowly, "I guess I just won't be able to take the class.''

Stephanie looked at Becky's sad face and gulped. All at once, she felt terrible. Becky was always doing favors for everybody in the family. And now, the one time Becky was asking for a favor from somebody else, Stephanie was letting her down. It just wasn't fair.

Besides that, Stephanie reminded herself, this would be her first real baby-sitting job. She didn't want to lose it. It was her big chance to prove to everyone in the house that she was as grown-up as D.J.

"Of course I can do the baby-sitting, Aunt Becky!" Stephanie said. "I mean, I'll figure out something for the committee meetings. Go ahead and take your class, and don't worry about a thing. Nicky and Alex are in good hands."

Becky stood up and gave her a big smile. "Are you sure, Steph?" she asked.

"Abso-positively!" Stephanie said.

"Well, thank you. This really means a lot to me. I've been looking forward to taking this class for a long time."

Becky turned around to pick up the boys and discovered they were both hiding under Michelle's bed. She got down on her hands and knees to pull them out. "Hey," she said. "There are actually some dust balls under here."

"Wow!" Stephanie said. "Dad will be *so* happy. Now he can use his latest Appliance of the Month Club selection." Danny Tanner was the resident neat freak.

"You mean the vacuum cleaner attachment," Becky asked, "with the heavy-duty beater-brush power head?"

"Yup," Stephanie said. "And the six-foot rotating extension."

"I'll go down and get him," Michelle said as

she trotted toward the door. "This is really going to make Dad's day."

Becky scooped up the twins and followed Michelle out of the room. "Thanks again about the baby-sitting, Steph!" she called over her shoulder.

"No problem!" Stephanie called back. Then she sighed. "No problem," she said again, "except for me and the sixth-grade project committee!"

She flopped back down on her bed and closed her eyes to concentrate on her problem. The next thing she knew she was awakened by the humming sound of a motor running. Realizing she'd drifted off to sleep, Stephanie rolled over and gazed across the room. Her father was crawling across the floor, vacuuming with a vengeance under Michelle's bed.

"Gotcha!" Danny exclaimed happily. "You thought you could escape me, didn't you, my little dust devil? But no one escapes the clutches of my new rotating power head! Ha, ha, ha!"

He sat up and saw Stephanie watching him. "Oh, hi, sweetie. You were so quiet, I didn't even notice you over there." He got to his feet. "Hey, would you like to try my new vacuum cleaner attachment under your bed? It's got a six-foot—"

"Rotating extension," Stephanie finished. "I know. Thanks but no thanks, Dad. Maybe some other time. Right now I'm concentrating on inventing a way of being two places at once!"

Danny looked puzzled. "Okay," he said. "I'll leave you alone so you can think in peace. Let me know if you want to talk about it." He started taking apart his rotating power head. "Would you like to vacuum together tomorrow night?"

"Yeah, Dad. Tomorrow. For sure."

But by lunchtime the next day, vacuuming was the furthest thing from Stephanie's mind. *What am I going to do?* she asked herself once again as she carried her tray across the cafeteria. *How can I clone myself so I can be at two places at the same time?*

"I just can't figure it out," she told Allie and Darcy as they sat down with their trays.

Darcy was staring at the food on her plate. "What's this stuff supposed to be, anyway?"

"Spaghetti?" Allie suggested doubtfully.

"It looks more like a hundred wiggling, giggling worms," Stephanie said absentmindedly. "Ho, ho, ho."

Allie and Darcy gaped at her. *"What?"* they both exclaimed.

Stephanie looked embarrassed. "Sorry," she said. "Michelle keeps singing this stupid song about worms, and I just can't get it out of my head."

"Wonderful," Darcy murmured. "Worms for lunch." She pushed her plate away. "So now that you've totally killed my appetite, Stephanie, I can concentrate on your problem."

"Give us the scenario one more time," Allie said. "Maybe we'll come up with an idea."

"It's like this," Stephanie said. "I promised Becky I'd baby-sit for Nicky and Alex every Tuesday afternoon for the next six weeks."

"And the next three Tuesdays are when you're supposed to be running the library fund-raising committee!" Darcy said.

"Right," Stephanie said. "I can't let Becky

down. But I also can't let the whole sixth grade down!" She groaned and rested her cheek on the cafeteria tabletop. "It's hopeless."

"We'll figure out something, Steph," Allie said, then turned to Darcy. "You can have half my sandwich," she offered, "if you're not going to finish that stuff on your plate. What do you think it *is*, anyway?"

"I've got it!" Darcy cried excitedly.

"You mean you've figured out what your lunch is?" Stephanie asked.

"No!" Darcy said. "I've figured out the answer to your problem! Allie and I will be your co-chairpeople. We can go to the meetings for you. After all, we're already on the committee."

Stephanie stared at her. "But . . ." she said slowly. "But is that really fair to you guys? I mean, you'd be doing all the work."

"No, we wouldn't," Darcy said, taking a bite out of Allie's sandwich. "You could still come up with a lot of the ideas. And you *know* we'll make you do a lot of the work once the project gets going."

"We'll just run the meetings," Allie added.

"And if there's a problem, we can call you at home. So what do you say, Steph?"

Stephanie sat up and let out a long, relieved breath. "I say thanks a bunch—and let's go for it!" She grinned at her friends. "You know something?" she said happily. "I think it's just possible this deal might work out after all!"

CHAPTER
3

◆ ◄ ◆ ◆

When Stephanie got home from school the next Tuesday, she met Joey, D.J., and Jesse all hurrying out the front door at once.

"Where's everybody going?" Stephanie asked.

Joey answered first. "I'm on my way to try out for a gig at a comedy club," he said. "I'm planning to do my impersonation of a creature that's a cross between a centipede and a parrot."

"What in the world does that sound like, Joey?" D.J. asked.

"A walkie-talkie!" Joey answered. He started making static noises in the back of his throat. *"Zzzzt. Phssst. Baruzzzzt!"*

Jesse rolled his eyes. "Don't quit your day job, Joey."

"This *is* my day job, Jess," Joey said in a hurt voice.

"So where are you going, Uncle Jesse?" Stephanie asked.

"The band's got a major rehearsal, Steph. We're putting on a Look Back at Elvis show next weekend, and we still haven't gotten all the bugs out of 'Hound Dog.' "

"Have you tried some of Comet's flea powder?" Joey asked.

"You *are* quite the comedian," Jesse told him.

D.J. looked at her watch. "I'm already late for meeting Steve," she said. "We're having a French study date. *Au revoir.*"

As she hurried down the front steps, Stephanie, Jesse, and Joey exchanged amused glances. D.J. and her boyfriend, Steve, were always claiming to have "study" dates. But the two of them were still so ga-ga over each other, no one in the family believed they actually got much studying done.

"Are you ready for your first big baby-sitting gig, Steph?" Jesse asked her.

"You bet," Stephanie said.

"Terrific," Jesse said. "Becky's inside waiting for you, with all the stuff you'll need for handling our two little monst—er—munchkins. I'm sure you'll do a great job." He reached over and ruffled the top of her long blond hair.

Stephanie grinned. She stood on tiptoe and tried to ruffle Jesse's hair. But her uncle caught her hand and said, "Not the hair, Steph! Don't mess with the hair!"

Joey was in a hurry to get going. "As the cow told the bull, Jess," he said, "it's time we got mooooving. Come on, and I'll give you a ride. Good luck, Stephanie!"

"Thanks, Joey."

Stephanie walked into the living room, where she crashed right into Michelle, who was parading around the room singing her worm song.

> *"One hundred giggling worms,*
> *Ho, ho, ho!*
> *One hundred wiggling worms,*
> *High and low!*
> *Oh, those wiggling, giggling worms,*
> *Watch them go!"*

Is she trying to drive me crazy? Stephanie asked herself. "I'll watch *you* go!" she said. "Right out the window—if you don't stop singing that silly song!"

"I *am* going," Michelle said. "Just as soon as Annie's mother comes to pick me up for our Honeybees meeting."

"Well, until she comes, Michelle, please, *please* sing something else!"

Michelle opened her mouth to begin a rousing chorus of "Baby Beluga." But at that moment, a harried Becky rushed into the living room and interrupted her. "Oh, thank goodness you're here, Steph!" she said. "The twins are in the kitchen begging for their afternoon snack, and I'm already running late. Please be sure and give Nicky his medicine for his ear infection at exactly four o'clock. It's already measured out."

Becky picked up her purse and a shiny new red notebook. "And you'd better not take them outside today because I think Alex is starting a cold, and it's still a little chilly. And try to keep track of Nicky's blankie because he gets hysterical if he can't find it. Whew! I think that's everything." She headed for the door. Then she turned around. "Are you sure you can manage, Steph?"

"Sure!" Stephanie said cheerfully.

"Then I'm outta here! Thanks a lot. I'll be back in a couple of hours." Becky opened the door and said, "Michelle, Annie's mother's out here waiting for you!" With a wave, she and Michelle left the house together.

Stephanie hurried into the kitchen, where she found Alex and Nicky patiently sitting at their little plastic picnic table. "Hi, guys!" she said. "Are you hungry?"

"Hung-wee!" Alex announced. "Want see-weal!"

"See-weal?" Stephanie repeated doubtfully.

Alex pointed to a box of Fruit Toastee-O's sitting on the counter. "See-weal!" he said.

"Oh!" Stephanie laughed. *"Cereal!* Sure thing." She opened the cupboard and got out two plastic Mickey Mouse bowls. "A double order of cereal coming right up." She took a brand-new carton of milk out of the refrigerator and opened it. Before she could pour it, the phone rang.

"Hold that thought, guys," she told the twins. "I'll be right back."

She ran to answer the phone. "Hello?"

"Hi, Steph. It's me, Darcy."

"Oh, hi, Darce. How's the meeting going?"

"Okay. I guess. . . . Well, if you want to know the truth, we're having a few problems."

"What's all that noise in the background?" Stephanie asked.

"That's the committee meeting!" Darcy said. "The kids we picked are really getting wild. Some of the boys are even making spitballs!"

"Oh, gosh!" Stephanie said. "How dumb can they be? Didn't anybody come up with an idea for the fund-raiser project?"

"That's why I'm calling you," Darcy said. "Christopher Ripple suggested a car wash. And Kara Landford wants to have a bake sale so she can make her aunt Edna's lemon poppyseed cake. Do you think those sound like good ideas?"

Crash! A tremendous thud came from behind Stephanie's back. *The twins!* she thought. "Gotta go, Darcy!" she said, banging the receiver back in place. Then she whirled around.

"Oh, *no!*" What are you guys doing?"

In the few minutes she'd been talking, Nicky had reached up onto the counter and knocked over the full carton of milk. Half the kitchen floor was now completely covered with milk. Nicky was sitting near a huge puddle, happily splashing his hands in the mess. Comet, the Tanner dog, was standing underneath the counter, waiting for the drips to fall into his mouth.

The other half of the kitchen floor was completely covered with Fruit Toastee-O's, which Alex had managed to open and dump out. Now he was happily eating the spilled cereal. He laughed as he scooped huge, sticky handfuls into his mouth.

"A milk flood," Stephanie said in dismay. "And a cereal landslide. You boys made a big *mess!* Comet, get out of here, please. And I mean *now!*"

While the dog ran out of the room, Stephanie stepped around the puddle of milk, crunched through the scattered Fruit Toastee-O's, and scooped up Alex. Holding him at arms' length, she crossed the room to the sink. She rinsed the crumbs of cereal off his hands and then wiped down his arms, face, clothes, hair, and knees. After that, she carried him to his high chair. While she was strapping him in, Nicky waded through the milk and started in on the Fruit Toastee-O's on the floor. Stephanie grabbed him and repeated the rinse and wipe routine at the sink.

When she finally had both twins buckled into their side-by-side high chairs, she cleaned up the milk flood. First, she sponged off the countertop. When that was finally done, she got out the mop and began working on the floor. She'd just started sweeping up the Fruit Toastee-O's when the phone rang again. She leaned the broom up against the wall and went to answer it. This time it was Allie.

"Hi, Stephanie. We're still over here at the library. But now we have another problem."

Behind her, the twins started yelling so loudly, Stephanie couldn't hear her friend's quiet voice. "What did you say, Allie? Could you speak up? I can't hear you!"

"I *said*," Allie repeated, "that Lizzie Timmons walked by the teachers' lounge, where the seventh-grade committee is having their project meeting. And she heard *them* talking about having a car wash and a bake sale, too. And everybody says we can't have the same project they're having. What do you think we should do?"

"Well, you know Mr. Mason said we should think big, and—"

"*Waaaahhhhhhh!*"

Stephanie whirled around and saw that Nicky and Alex had both grabbed the broom handle and were having a game of tug-of-war with it.

"Guys, no!" she said, hanging up with a bang. She grabbed the broom away from the twins and gave them each a book to look at.

"Hung-wee!" Nicky cried, throwing down the book.

Alex did the same, saying, "Want see-weal!"

Wearily, Stephanie started across the room for clean bowls and walked right through the pile of Fruit Toastee-O's she'd just swept up. Little lemon-, grape-, lime-, and raspberry-colored O's rolled across the clean floor.

At that very instant, the back door opened. D.J.'s friend Kimmy stuck her head into the kitchen.

"Yoo-hoo! Anybody home?" she called.

That's all I need, Stephanie thought. *If Kimmy tells everybody about this mess, my family will never believe I can handle a baby-sitting job!*

"No one's home, Kimmy," Stephanie answered shortly.

Kimmy ignored her. "I was wondering if D.J. was here yet," she said, walking into the house. "I thought we might par-lay voo a little French, and—" She abruptly stopped talking when she noticed the mess on the kitchen floor. "What happened in *here?*" she asked in amazement.

Stephanie put her hands on her hips. "Nothing," she replied firmly. "Absolutely nothing. And if you tell anybody anything different, Kimmy, I'll tell D.J. you're the one who borrowed her new black leggings without even asking and then washed them in hot water so they shrank down to the size of a Barbie outfit!"

"Okay, okay," Kimmy said hastily. "You don't have to get nasty. I didn't see a thing."

"And D.J.'s off on a so-called study date with Steve," Stephanie added. "So there's not much point in waiting around, unless you want to help me clean up this place, or—"

"Gotta run!" Kimmy said, backing out the door. "But I think I might drop back in at dinnertime. Looking at all this food has made me really hungry."

"Hung-wee!" Alex squealed as Kimmy closed the door. He pointed at the cereal on the floor. "See-weal. Me want!"

"Those are all dirty," Stephanie said, scraping crushed cereal off the bottom of her shoe. "I'll see what else we have." She opened up the cupboard. "Let's see. Do you like oat bran? Whole-grain granola? Swedish-recipe Müeslix?"

"No, no!" both boys shouted.

Stephanie stared at the screaming boys. For a wild moment, she wanted to run out the back door.

"Get a grip!" she said out loud. Then she started suggesting other snacks. Finally, they all agreed on some small bowls of pizza-flavored crackers shaped like different kinds of bugs.

Stephanie sighed with relief. "Okay, guys. You can be froggies and eat up the little buggies."

"Fwoggy!" Alex shouted. "Ribbit. Hop! Hop! Out! Out!"

"Out! Out!" Nicky echoed.

Forgetting all about their snacks, both twins started struggling to get out of their high chairs so they could get down on the floor and be frogs. With another sigh, Stephanie unfastened their straps and helped them climb out. Immediately both boys shouted, "Ribbit! Ribbit!" and frog-hopped out of the room. With a groan, Stephanie went after them.

After several minutes of Chase the Frog Around the Living Room Couch, Stephanie managed to get Nicky and Alex onto the couch to look at a book. They were in the middle of *Runaway Bunny* when the phone interrupted them.

"Hi, Steph! It's Darcy again. Kara says she's going to quit the committee if we don't let her make her lemon poppyseed cake for the bake sale. What do you think we should do?"

When she spoke, Stephanie's voice sounded slightly hysterical. "I don't even think we should *have* a bake sale!"

"Well, you don't have to shout, Stephanie. All I wanted to know was what you thought we should—"

"Maaaaamaaaaaa!"

Stephanie winced. Then she turned around and saw that Alex had grabbed Nicky's hair and started to pull. *"Owwwwwww!"* Nicky said.

Once again, she slammed down the phone and ran to rescue Nicky. As she went, she noticed that the time on the digital clock said four forty-five.

Oh, no! Stephanie thought. *Now I've really messed up. Nicky was supposed to have his medicine forty-five minutes ago!*

She pulled Alex off his brother and carried a screaming Nicky into the kitchen. "You're okay, Nicky," she said soothingly, giving him a hug. "And now it's time for your pink medicine."

"Want bankie. Want bankie."

"Bankie? You want a piggy bank?"

"Nooooo! Want *bankie! Waahhhhhh!*"

Stephanie cast a wild-eyed look around the kitchen, desperately trying to figure out what Nicky was talking about. All at once, she remembered Becky's instructions.

"You want your blankie!"

Nicky smiled at her and nodded. "Bankie," he agreed.

39

Stephanie put him down and started looking under every table, chair, and counter.

"I give up, Nicky," she said after a long, frantic search. "Your blankie simply isn't in here anymore. It must be upstairs."

Nicky toddled across the room and pointed at Danny's gardening galoshes, which were standing just inside the back door. He reached in one of the big black boots and pulled out his well-worn, faded blue flannel blanket.

Stephanie shook her head. "I can't believe it. You knew where it was the whole time."

Nicky hugged the blanket to his chest and gave her a big, sweet smile. Stephanie picked him up and helped him drink his dose of medicine. Then she hastily swept up the rest of the Fruit Toastee-O's. As she carried Nicky back into the living room, she saw that Alex was standing up on the couch.

"Be careful," she said. "You could fall."

As she spoke, Alex lost his balance, and at the same instant, the phone rang again.

Stephanie put Nicky down, grabbed Alex just before he was about to fall, and ran to answer the phone.

"Hi, Stephanie, it's me, Darcy, again."

Alex stopped crying, yanked the phone away from Stephanie, and promptly hung it up. Two seconds later, it rang again.

"Shut up!" she screamed at the telephone. Then she smacked her forehead. "Oh, terrific. Now I'm yelling at the telephone. I must be going out of my mind!"

She put Alex down and reached out to answer the phone one more time. As she did, she spoke out loud. "How?" she asked the room. "How am I ever, *ever* going to be able to deal with this craziness for five more Tuesday afternoons?"

CHAPTER
4

◆ ◀ ◆ ◆

Stephanie had just managed to get the twins organized into a quiet game of Knock Down the Block Tower when Becky came home.

"Hi, boys!" she said. "Hi, Steph!"

"Mama!" squealed Nicky and Alex. They tumbled over each other in their hurry to get to their mother and grab her around the knees.

"Hello, you little cuties," she said. She tossed aside her notebook and purse, then bent down and smothered the boys with kisses. "Were you good boys? How did everything go, Stephanie?"

Stephanie thought fast. *If I tell the truth*, she told herself, *Becky will probably fire me on the spot.*

Then Dad and everybody else will think I'm unbelievably babyish. What should I do?

She opened her mouth and started talking. "Uh, well," she began. "Actually, to be completely accurate, everything went just fine. We had a little snack of cereal—"

"See-weal!" Alex shouted. "See-weal!"

"Milk!" Nicky chimed in. "Milk!"

Becky looked puzzled. "Are you guys asking for milk and cereal?" She turned to Stephanie. "Didn't they finish their snack?"

Stephanie felt her cheeks turning red. "Uh, yes. Yes, they did," she said quickly. "They had quite a big snack, as a matter of fact. Um, don't you two guys want to get back to our block-tower game now? I promise I'll make a really big one for you to knock down."

"Big tower," Alex said. "Big 'nack. Big *mess!*"

"Come on!" Stephanie broke in. "Let's make a big, *big* tower now, so you guys can smash it over. Okay?" She hurried to the block pile and started quickly building a huge, wobbly building. Alex and Nicky toddled after her. Before Stephanie could put on one more block, Alex smashed the tower to smithereens.

"More!" he yelled. "More towah!"

Becky got to her feet and picked up the purse and notebook she'd tossed on the floor. "Well, I can't thank you enough, Stephanie. It looks like you did a terrific job with the boys." She started toward the kitchen. "I think I'll go make myself some coffee and see if Joey left a note about what he wants to have for dinner."

Stephanie, who was busily piling up another block tower, called casually over her shoulder, "By the way, Becky, how was your class?"

"Oh, it was just fantastic!"

"So . . . you're not thinking of dropping out or anything?"

"Not at all," Becky answered. "I just loved it. I can't wait to go back next week. It was fantastic."

"And you really think you can handle all the homework along with your busy work schedule and the twins and everything?"

"That's the terrific thing, Steph," Becky said as she went into the kitchen. "The instructor told us today there isn't going to be any homework at all. Isn't that amazing?"

"Amazing," Stephanie muttered under her breath. "Just fantastic."

She was still brooding when Joey opened the front door a few minutes later. "Hey, Stephanie," he said as he came in. "The house is still standing. That must mean you had a successful baby-sitting experience. How'd it go?"

"Okay, I guess," Stephanie said. "How was your audition? Did you get the job?"

"Yes, I did!" Joey answered happily. "Listen to this joke I told them: A teacher said to a little boy, 'Where's your pencil, Tommy?'

"So Tommy answered, 'I ain't got none.'

"So the teacher said, 'How many times do I have to tell you not to say that, Tommy? Now listen: I do not have a pencil. You do not have a pencil. They do not have a pencil. Do you understand now, Tommy?'

" 'Not really,' says Tommy. 'I mean, what happened to all the pencils?' "

Joey slapped his knee. "I really killed them with that one," he said. "Sometimes I just crack myself right up!" He laughed again, then stared at Stephanie, who was staring back at him with a blank expression. "If you don't mind my saying so, Steph, you seem to be slightly under-whelmed by my joke. Do you want me to tell you another one to cheer you up?"

Stephanie sighed. "No, thanks, Joey. I guess I'm just not in the mood for humor right now. Sorry if I didn't appreciate your joke."

"That's okay," Joey said. "I'm sure you'll cheer up after dinner. Tonight I'm making my famous four-cheese macaroni with breadcrumbs on top. You always say it's your favorite."

But even four-cheese macaroni couldn't help cheer up Stephanie. And her mood didn't get any better the next day when she found out what had happened the day before at the sixth-grade committee meeting in the library. She was getting her social studies book out of her locker when Darcy and Allie hurried up to her.

"Stephanie!" Darcy said. "You absolutely can-not miss another committee meeting. This one was a total disaster without you."

"The pits," Allie agreed. "I hate to say it, but it was a real catastrophe."

Stephanie banged shut her locker. "How bad could it have been?" she asked. "I mean, what exactly happened?"

Allie looked at Darcy and rolled her eyes. "What *didn't* happen? You tell her, Darcy."

"I'll tell you what didn't happen," Darcy said. "We *didn't* come up with any good ideas for the sixth-grade project!"

"No one could think of anything interesting at all," Allie said. "And the few ideas we did come up with have already been taken by the seventh graders."

"And then everybody started complaining and whining," Darcy went on. "And a lot of kids were just acting silly and goofing off! And then Kara Landford said the whole committee was stupid, and she wasn't sure she wanted to be a part of it. After that, a bunch of the kids said they were thinking about quitting the committee altogether!"

Stephanie groaned. "I'm beginning to think those kids might have the right idea," she said. "This whole project *is* turning out to be a disaster. Maybe we should just go tell Mr. Mason we can't—"

"Hey, Stephanie! Darcy! Allie!"

The three girls turned their heads. They all gasped. Josh Hillman, Caleb Parker, and the new boy, Ron Martinez, were walking down the hall. They were coming right toward them!

Suddenly Stephanie started worrying about how she looked. *Oh, no,* she thought. *Why didn't I wear that new shiny Forty-Niners jacket I got at the mall last week? Why was I so bummed out this morning that I stuck on this plain old gray T-shirt with the frayed collar?*

"We just heard about the sixth-grade thing for the library," Josh called to Stephanie. "Are you on the committee?"

"Uh, yes," Stephanie said. "Yes, I am. And so are Darcy and Allie."

Allie, who was very shy with boys, looked like she wanted to open a locker and crawl inside. But Darcy flashed her biggest, most beautiful smile at Caleb. "We're the three co-chairpeople," she said. "We're trying to come up with some good ideas for our project."

"Well, we're hoping you'll come up with some *great* ideas!" Caleb told her.

"Right," Ron added. "All the guys on the soccer team have been talking about it. We think a day off for a class picnic would be super."

"We're counting on you three, Stephanie,"

Josh put in. "We're sure you guys can come up with something that will really blow away the seventh and eighth graders."

Stephanie gulped. She struggled to make her voice sound normal. "Oh, you can count on us, Josh," she said, trying not to stare at his extra-long curly eyelashes. "We have so many fantastic ideas, we can't decide which one to pick!"

"For sure?" Josh asked.

"No lie," Stephanie gushed. "We'll make the most money in the whole school—without a doubt."

"Well, we hope so," Caleb said. "Because if the sixth grade *doesn't* win, then we'll know who to blame!"

The three boys laughed and strolled off down the hall.

"How rude!" Stephanie said. "Why don't they join the committee if they're so wild to win the day off?"

"Stephanie," Allie pleaded. "Don't you see? Now we *have* to win that day off—or else everybody in school will be going around saying what a bunch of losers we are."

"She's right, Steph," Darcy said. "Without you and your ideas, we're lost on that committee. You just have to come to the next meeting."

"I know you're right," Stephanie said. "But how am I supposed to do that without letting Becky down and making her think I'm the lowest form of life on the planet?"

CHAPTER
5

◆ ◢ ◆ ◆

The next Tuesday morning, when Stephanie got out of bed, she tried to get into a good mood by putting on one of her favorite outfits. But even her lavender T-shirt, matching miniskirt, and cowboy boots failed to cheer her up. She frowned at her reflection in the mirror and stuck out her tongue. Then she stomped downstairs and into the kitchen. She found the rest of her family cheerfully chattering around the breakfast table.

D.J. was busily practicing her French on everyone. *"J'en voudrais encore,"* she said, reaching for another waffle from the platter on the table.

"I know some tongue twisters too," Michelle

51

said with a mouthful of oatmeal. "Rubber baby buggy bumpers. Rugger bubby bamby boopers. See?"

"That's cute, Michelle," Danny told her. "But do you think you could make an extra effort not to drool oatmeal onto the kitchen floor today? I just washed and waxed it last night, and believe me, it wasn't easy. Some kind of strange grainy red, yellow, purple, and green substance had been ground into the tiles!"

Stephanie remembered the Fruit Toastee-O's and avoided looking at Nicky and Alex. The twins were quietly sitting in their side-by-side high chairs, busily mashing their bowls of sliced banana into mushy pulps. Becky, who was trying to feed them, was wearing a full-length plastic apron and a shower cap to protect herself from the mess.

"Fortunately," Danny went on, "my latest appliance of the month arrived yesterday, and let me tell you, it is one dandy of an invention. By remarkable coincidence, it turned out to be a rotating floor polisher. One turn of the switch, and that baby buffed those mysterious little grains right out of existence! I called Vicky and told her all about it last night. She was simply fascinated."

Vicky was Danny's fiancée from Chicago. They'd met when Vicky had replaced Becky as the co-host of *Wake Up, San Francisco* when Becky was on maternity leave. Now Vicky was back in Chicago, and she and Danny were conducting a long-distance romance.

The back door opened, and Kimmy Gibbler walked in.

"*Bonjour*, Kimmy," D.J. said. "*Petit déjeuner?*"

"I don't know what you said, Deej," Kimmy answered. "But if you asked if I've had breakfast yet, the answer is yes. If you asked if I want to have a second breakfast, the answer is also yes." She pulled out a chair, sat down at the table, and helped herself to a waffle from the serving platter.

Belting out an Elvis hit called "Little Sister," Jesse bounded down the stairs and struck a dramatic pose in the middle of the kitchen. "What do you think of the outfit, ladies and gentlemen?"

Comet barked, and everyone turned around to gaze in wonder at Jesse. He was wearing a complete Elvis outfit, including a shiny, spangled silver shirt, a huge gold belt buckle, fringed pants, and boots. Even his beloved hair was moussed up into a high, pouffy, Elvis-style do.

"It's magnificent, Jess," Joey said from the end of the table. "But isn't it just a little early in the year for Halloween costumes?"

"Very funny, Joey," Jesse responded. He paused in front of the mirror and carefully ran a hand over the top of his glossy hair. "But I'm not going trick or treating. The band is rehearsing all day for the Look Back at Elvis show we are doing next weekend. We thought wearing the appropriate clothing might help us get into the true spirit of the music." He grinned at his reflection. "You know, dressed like this, I am an absolute twin for the King of Rock and Roll."

"Speaking of twins, how about helping me out with these little guys right now?" Becky asked him. "They're taking forever to eat, and I have to leave for the studio."

Jesse stared down at the boys' food-encrusted hands and faces. "Feed the rug rats?" he asked in dismay. "And risk messing up the outfit?"

Becky untied the apron and took off the

shower cap. Underneath, she was wearing a linen suit. "Here," she said. She handed the cap and apron to Jesse. "You can borrow these."

Jesse sighed and slowly started strapping on the protective gear. "I'll put on the apron," he said grimly. "But no way am I putting that cap on this hair."

Becky laughed and gave him a quick kiss on the cheek. Then she went to the back door and opened it. "My goodness!" she exclaimed. "It's beautiful out today. You know something, Stephanie? I think you could take the twins out this afternoon. They're over their colds, and it would be good for them to get some fresh air."

Stephanie, who'd been stabbing her eggs in gloomy silence, suddenly looked up. "You're saying you want me to take Nicky and Alex out this afternoon?" she asked.

Danny looked puzzled. "Is there an echo in here?" he said. "Isn't that what Becky just told you, honey?"

"*Déjà vu*," D.J. said.

"*Gesundheit*," Kimmy replied.

"Pater Peeper pecked a pick of peppled pippers!" Michelle piped up.

"Yikes!" Jesse screamed, backing away from the twins. "You guys are supposed to be *eating* your bananas, not wearing them in your hair!"

Becky stopped in front of the mirror to put on lipstick. Then she ran a comb through her long dark hair.

"Sure, Steph," she said as she picked up her purse. "You could take them to that little playground up the block. You know—the one with the chain-link fence all around it so the kids can't escape?"

Danny smiled. "How well I know that little playground," he said. "I used to take you there, Stephanie, when you were two. And now, look at you—ready to take on the responsibilities of a full-fledged baby-sitter! Time is passing so quickly." He looked at his watch and frowned. "In fact," he said, getting to his feet, "it's passing a lot more quickly than I thought. We'd better hurry, Becky, or we're going to be late getting to the studio this morning."

Becky and Danny kissed everyone good-bye and left for work. A few minutes later, Stephanie picked up her books and headed for the bus stop. As she walked, she hummed a little tune to herself. Although she didn't realize it, the song sounded an awful lot like Michelle's "One Hundred Giggling Worms." She was too pleased with herself to notice what she was singing. Mysteriously, her bad mood had vanished. Something Becky had said at breakfast had given her an idea. Now Stephanie had a Plan.

As soon as Becky left for her film-editing class later that afternoon, Stephanie put the Plan into action. The instant the door was closed, she whipped out the twins' little hats and jackets.

"Okay, guys," she told them. "We're going outside."

"Out-tide!" yelled Nicky. "Pway-gwound!"

"Well, not exactly," Stephanie said. "After all, you don't want to waste your whole life at some babyish playground, do you? Wouldn't you rather go see a big kids' school?"

"Skoo!" Alex shouted. "See skoo!"

"See skoo!" Nicky repeated.

"See? They *want* to go!" Stephanie said to herself. "It'll be an educational experience. After all, Becky did say I should take them out today." As she spoke, she tried to ignore the little pangs of guilt she was feeling. In her heart, she knew that Becky would be less than thrilled at what she was about to do. But she didn't want to think about that right now. Right now, she was determined to carry out the Plan.

She finished wrestling the twins into their hats and jackets and strapped them into their double stroller. Then she left the house and started half-jogging up the street. It was a long walk—more like run—to the school, but Stephanie wouldn't be able to get the double stroller on the bus. Twenty minutes later, she pushed the stroller into the school library.

She was met by the sound of six or seven voices talking, all at once.

"But everybody simply adores my lemon poppyseed cake," Kara Landford whined. "I don't understand why you don't want to have a bake sale."

"Why can't we have a car wash?" Christopher Ripple asked. "Just because the seventh graders are having one doesn't mean we can't have one too."

"What if we just went around with a can

58

and asked for donations?'' Lizzie Timmons suggested.

"Or better yet," another boy put in, "what if we all just went home right now? We're not getting anywhere. This committee is totally bogus.''

"Ditto!" said someone else.

Allie, who was sitting in the back of the room, hid her face in her hands.

"Order!" Darcy shouted. "Please sit down and come to order.''

Just then, Kara noticed Stephanie standing in the doorway. "Ohhhh!" she squealed. "Are those your little twin cousins? Aren't they just too adorable? Can we play with them?''

"I guess so," Stephanie said doubtfully. "But . . ." Before she could finish speaking, Kara had darted across the room and lifted Nicky and Alex out of the stroller. Christopher Ripple followed her.

"I just love little kids," he said. He bulged out his cheeks and made a goofy face at Alex.

The toddler burst out laughing. "More!" he cried. "More face!''

"Oh, I can do better than that," said Chris.

He got down on his hands and knees and stuck out his tongue. "Woof!" he said. "Bowwow! I'm a dog, see?"

Alex came over and patted him on the head. "Doggy!" he said in delight. "Bowwow!"

Chris was thrilled. "Hey!" he exclaimed. "I'm good at this. I should be a clown."

Meanwhile Kara had placed Nicky on a chair and started teaching him "The Eensy-Weensy Spider." He was crowing with delight as he tried to imitate her wiggling hand motions.

"This is soooo much fun," Kara said. "I just adore playing games with these little angels."

"That's nice," Darcy said. "But we still haven't come up with any ideas for the fund-raiser!"

Stephanie clapped her hands together and screamed, "That's *it!*"

Everyone turned around and stared at her. "What's it, Steph?" Allie asked.

"The idea! For our project. We can have a carnival. For all the little kids!"

"Wow, Stephanie," Darcy said. "That sounds like it could be a great project. But how would it work?"

Stephanie eagerly came forward and sat down at the table. She brought out a pencil and paper and started scribbling notes. "Well," she began, "you remember how the parents are also having a library fund-raiser the same day as ours?"

"Right," said Darcy. "They're having some kind of auction in the gym."

"You got it," Stephanie continued. "So what if we have our carnival out on the playground? While the parents are busy inside the school, we can be baby-sitters for the little kids outside! That way, we can charge the parents an admission fee they'll be more than happy to pay."

"Awesome!" Chris said. "Can I be a clown?"

"Sure," Stephanie said. She made a note on her paper. "What else should we have?"

"Well, food of course," said Kara. "I'll be in charge of that. I can bring some of my—"

"Lemon poppyseed cake," Darcy finished. "But you'd better bring some chocolate-chip cookies, too. And lemonade. And other stuff little kids like."

"What about face painting?" Lizzie suggested. "I always loved that when I was a little kid. And maybe an arts and crafts table?"

"Great ideas!" Stephanie said, writing furiously.

"We could have an obstacle course," put in another boy. "And games—like Leapfrog."

"And Duck Duck Goose!" said someone else. "And a cakewalk with a wheel of fortune where the kids can spin a wheel and win a cake if the pointer stops on their number."

"What about setting up a little basketball hoop for the kids to shoot at?"

"Or one of those fish pond booths where the kids fish for little prizes from behind a screen?"

"What about a plastic bowling game?"

"Terrific!" Stephanie cried, making more and more notes. "Keep going!"

Before long, the committee members were suggesting ideas so fast, it was all Stephanie could do to write every one down. Finally, after half an hour of loud talking, the room got quiet.

Stephanie let out a long breath. "Whew!" she said. "Now let's see if I've got this straight. Everyone knows who they're going to ask to donate stuff, like cooking ingredients, art supplies, and sports and game equipment, right?"

"Right!" everyone agreed.

"And each one of us is going to ask at least two people from our class to help with jobs like building booths, making food, running the carnival, and selling tickets?"

"Right!"

"Fantastic," Stephanie said. "That makes eighteen of us altogether. Are there any other ideas?"

"Well, I did have one idea for a kind of creature feature booth," Kara said. "What if we put a giant T-shirt on your little twin cousins and billed them as a two-headed space alien?"

Stephanie stared at her. "Somehow, Kara," she replied slowly, "somehow I just don't think my aunt and uncle will go for that. But thanks for the suggestion anyway."

"Don't mention it," Kara replied.

"I just can't believe you came up with such a brilliant idea, Steph," Darcy said. "But what about the eighth graders? What about the brilliant idea they keep hinting around about? Has anybody been able to find out what it is?"

"I keep trying," Allie admitted. "Whenever I see a bunch of eighth graders whispering in the halls, I sneak up behind them, but somehow they always seem to know I'm there!"

"They have eyes in the backs of their heads," said Chris.

"Maybe we could exhibit *them* as space aliens!" Stephanie joked. Everybody laughed.

"Why do you think they're making such a big deal out of keeping it a secret?" Darcy asked.

"Jenni probably thinks we'd try to steal their idea," Stephanie said. "How dumb! As if we'd sink so low."

"Who needs their idea?" Allie said. "Now we have a great idea of our own!"

"Right!" everybody chorused.

"A baby-sitting carnival is the best idea ever, Stephanie!" Darcy said.

"If I do say so myself," Stephanie said modestly, "I have to agree with you." She looked around the library. Then she jumped up. "Speaking of baby-sitting," she cried in alarm, "where are Nicky and Alex?"

"They're over here behind the biography section," said Chris. "They're okay. They're just . . . uh-oh."

Stephanie jumped up and ran around the

bookshelf next to the table. Nick and Alex were sitting in the middle of the floor, happily ripping pages out of two thick biographies of George Washington.

"Oh, gosh!" she exclaimed. "No, no ripping books, boys!" She grabbed the biographies and stuffed them into her backpack. "Wait till Mr. Mason sees these!" she muttered to herself. "I just hope he doesn't call Dad and tell him how irresponsible I was."

Before the twins could get into any more trouble, she scooped them up and put them back into their stroller. Then she announced, "Today's meeting is adjourned. This committee meets again next week: same time, same place."

She glanced at her watch and gasped. She had exactly nineteen minutes to get back home with the boys before Becky returned from her class!

CHAPTER
6

◆ ◀ ◆ ◆

A panting, gasping Stephanie reached home with only a few minutes to spare. She was just taking off the twins' hats and jackets when Becky came through the front door.

"Alex!" she cried, giving both boys big hugs. "Nicky! Hello!"

Becky took off her jacket and hung it in the closet. "I see you took them out today. How'd it go?"

"Uh," Stephanie began. "Uh, just fine."

"Go!" Nicky yelled. "Go out!"

"Skoo!" Alex chimed in. "Skoo! See book! See book!"

Becky smiled at the boys. "Did you hear how

clearly Alex just said *book*, Steph? I guess that means you spent some time reading to them today. You're really turning out to be a terrific baby-sitter!"

Stephanie felt her cheeks turning red. "Well, I guess you could say we spent some time with books today," she mumbled. *This is a big pain*, she thought. *Telling half the truth all the time is really turning out to be hard!*

"What do you think this 'skoo' is that Alex is so excited about?" Becky continued. "Do you think he might be talking about a character from one of the books you read?"

Stephanie knew perfectly well that Alex was trying to say *school*. But obviously she couldn't admit that to Becky without giving away the secret of where she'd taken the boys. All she could do was shrug and give a little smile. "Maybe," she said. "Maybe that's it."

That night at dinner, she felt even more ashamed about the secret she was keeping from her family. Becky praised her baby-sitting skills for so long that Stephanie wanted to sink through the floor and disappear.

"Not only did she take the boys out in the

fresh air today!" Becky raved. "But she also found time to read to them. Why, Alex and Nicky couldn't wait to tell me all about it!"

"My little girl is really growing up and becoming a responsible adult," Danny said proudly.

"Give me five!" said Jesse, raising his hand for a high five. "If you have survived my offspring, you can survive anything!"

"*Magnifique!*" said D.J.

"Mmmffbloflix," Kimmy mumbled. As usual, she'd conveniently "happened" to drop by the house at dinnertime. Her mouth was full of mashed potatoes, and it was difficult to understand exactly what she was saying.

Stephanie, who couldn't believe the way everyone was carrying on, fought the urge to clap her hands over her ears. She desperately wanted to tell them all about the neat idea she'd come up with for the sixth-grade project. But she knew she couldn't do that without telling them the whole truth.

Instead, she pushed her chair away from the table. "Thanks for all the compliments, everybody," she said quietly. "But it really wasn't such a big deal." She got to her feet. "Excuse

me, but I have an awful lot of homework tonight. I'll be upstairs in my room if anybody
wants me."

The next day at school, everyone on the sixth-
grade committee was still excited about the carnival idea. The kids were so psyched, it was
easy for Stephanie to stop thinking about the
way she'd fooled Becky.

Stephanie felt even happier at lunchtime,
when Allie and Darcy met her at their favorite
table in the cafeteria. "You know what I heard?"
Allie said. "I heard that Christopher Ripple
from our committee is friends with Ron from
the soccer team. And Chris told Ron about your
carnival idea, and Ron told all the other boys
on the team." She paused to take a breath.

"And?" Stephanie prompted. *"And?"*

"And, well, they all thought it was a good
idea, I guess."

"It *is* a good idea," Darcy said loyally.

All at once, they heard loud peals of laughter
coming from a nearby table. They turned
around and saw Jenni Morris, Diana Rink, and
several other eighth-grade Flamingoes staring

right at them. The older girls were giggling as if they were in on the biggest private joke in the world.

When Jenni saw Stephanie and her friends looking at her, she smirked. Then she turned around and whispered something to the other Flamingoes. They all looked over at Stephanie's table again and shrieked with uncontrollable laughter.

"Those girls go beyond rude," Stephanie said angrily. "What *do* they think is so funny?"

"I've heard the eighth graders have a really unbelievable project planned," Darcy said glumly. "Apparently it's something so good, they're saying no other class even has a chance of winning."

"It's better than a carnival?" Allie asked in disbelief.

"That's what everyone's saying," Darcy said. "But they're still keeping it a big secret."

"What could it be?" Stephanie wondered. "What could be that good?"

As the girls carried their trays over to the cleanup window, Josh Hillman and Caleb Parker came up to them.

"Hi, co-chairpeople," Josh said. He smiled at Stephanie, and she felt her heart begin to beat faster. She smiled back at him.

"We've heard you came up with an idea for our class's project," Caleb said. "It doesn't sound half-bad. But it does sound like a lot of work. Do you think you can pull it off?"

"I think *we* can pull it off!" Stephanie retorted. "If everybody in the class helps. After all, it is supposed to be a project for the whole class!"

"Well, we want to be sure it works out," Josh told her. "Because we're really counting on that day off from school."

"Hey, the carnival would be a great time for you guys to show your stuff," Stephanie told them. "You could bring a ball and play a game of soccer with the kids."

Josh and Caleb didn't know what to say to that, and Stephanie walked away wondering why the boys had to put so much pressure on her.

For the rest of the week at school, she and Darcy and Allie had to deal with Jenni and Diana's constant giggling and whispering behind their backs. They also received several more "hints" from Josh, Caleb, and Ron. The sixth-grade boys had spread the word that they would be very upset if their class's project didn't raise the most money for the library. But they had said nothing about helping with the carnival themselves.

By the following Tuesday afternoon, Stephanie was a nervous wreck. But that didn't stop her from using the Plan one more time. The moment Becky left for her film-editing class, Stephanie bundled the twins into the stroller again and ran all the way to the school library. She had no time to waste—the carnival was this coming Saturday and there was lots to do.

"Hi," Darcy said as Stephanie hurried in and unloaded Nicky and Alex. "We're just getting started."

"Great," Stephanie said breathlessly. "Let's hear what everybody has to report. Chris?"

"Well, I found a couple of other kids who said they want to be clowns with me. And Bonnie Tyler's mom said her boutique will donate free helium balloons for us to sell."

"Great!" Stephanie said, checking off an item on one of her many lists. "Kara?"

"I've got a lot of kids who are willing to bake cookies, homemade pretzels, or cakes or pies. Their parents say they'll kick in for all the ingredients."

"All right! Lizzie?"

"I talked to Harry Lamont, whose grandfather owns that discount store," Lizzie said. "He gave me a whole mess of paint and glue and cardboard and wood, and we loaded up our van, and it's all right—"

Lizzie stopped talking when Allie ran into the room. "I found out!" Allie gasped. "I found out what the eighth graders are doing for their fund-raiser!"

She threw herself into a chair and tried to catch her breath. Everyone else jumped up and surrounded her.

"Well?" Kara demanded. "What are they doing?"

"Oh, gosh," Allie said. "I hate to even tell you guys."

"Tell us, Allie!" Stephanie demanded. "Tell us *now!*"

"The eighth graders have gotten a real live movie star to help with their fund-raiser. They're going to charge people money to have their picture taken with her!"

"A movie star?" Darcy repeated. "Who is it?"

"Dara Dean!" Allie said. "Can you believe it?"

"Dara Dean!" Stephanie said in horror. "But . . . but . . . she's famous. And beautiful!"

"Well, that does it!" said Lizzie. "We might as well give up right now. We don't have a chance. I'm quitting the committee."

"You can't quit!" Darcy told her.

"Who says I can't?" Lizzie retorted. "Remember—I volunteered for this job!"

"Maybe we should come up with another idea," someone suggested.

"Isn't it kind of late for that?" said somebody else. "I already put in a lot of work on this carnival thing. I don't feel like starting all over again."

"Hey, this date stamp makes a great tattoo," a boy said from behind Mr. Mason's desk. "Let's stamp the date on our foreheads."

"Good idea," said another boy. "But let's make it for the year 2095!"

Stephanie couldn't believe what was happening. She slumped in her chair and grew more depressed by the minute. As she watched, the whole committee was falling apart in front of her very eyes. Her wonderful carnival idea was doomed!

"Let's go see if we can get sodas out of the machine in the teachers' lounge," Christopher suggested. "Sometimes if you kick it just right, all your money falls back out of the coin return."

"Let's go!" said another boy. He got up and started to follow Chris out of the room.

"WAIT A MINUTE!" Kara Landford stood up on a chair and shouted at the top of her lungs. "I HAVE AN IDEA!"

"She probably wants us to sell her lemon poppyseed cake door-to-door," Darcy whispered to Stephanie.

Kara glared at her. "I heard that, Darcy. But that is not my idea. My idea involves our chairperson, Stephanie." She climbed down from her chair and walked over to where Stephanie was sitting. "Stephanie, you're always bragging about how your father is on TV. Can't he get *us* somebody famous to come to the carnival?"

Stephanie flushed. "I don't think I really brag about my dad, Kara—" she began.

"Whatever," Kara interrupted. "That's not my point. What I'm saying is, why can't your father find us a big star like Dara Dean?"

"Well, he doesn't really like to ask favors from the people who come on his show," Stephanie said. "And a lot of times they're only in town for a day or so. Or else they're not really that famous. Like just the other day he interviewed the lizard expert from the San Francisco Zoo. I mean, nobody would pay to have their picture taken with that guy."

Kara moved a little closer to her. "But your father does know some celebrities, doesn't he?" she asked.

"Well, yes," Stephanie admitted, feeling more and more flustered. "But . . ."

"So why couldn't you just go home and ask him to at least *try* to get us one?"

At that point, several other kids joined the argument. "Yeah, why couldn't you, Stephanie?" they asked. "Couldn't you at least try? Don't you want us to win the day off?"

By now, the pressure was making Stephanie feel completely desperate. Suddenly she just blurted something out. "I have a different idea!" she exclaimed. "A better idea. I can get us a real rock band!" She thought of Uncle Jesse and prayed she could convince him to do this favor for her. If he did, she'd promise to be his faithful servant for the rest of his life.

"A rock band?" Kara asked. "Do you know rock stars?"

"Well, it's only my uncle, but he *is* a professional musician," Stephanie explained. "And his band is really great."

"Do they play requests?" Chris asked.

"Yeah," said Stephanie. "Especially if it's Elvis or the Beach Boys."

"That would get everybody dancing," Allie said. "And we'd attract all kinds of attention. What a cool idea, Steph."

"I think so too," Darcy said.

After the excited kids had quieted down a bit, Darcy continued. "I also think we'd better get to work or we'll never be ready in time. Lizzie, didn't you start to tell us you have a big load of art supplies for us to use for booths and props and things?"

"Right," Lizzie said. "It's right out in the hall. I guess we'd better haul it down to the gym and get to work in there."

Several kids followed Lizzie out the door. Soon they were carrying cans of paint, paint-brushes, and big sheets of cardboard down the hall to the gym. Stephanie was picking up her papers and studying her lists when Alex wandered up to her.

"Paint!" he said. "Paint!"

"Oh, no!" Stephanie cried as she looked at him. Somehow, without anyone noticing, Alex had gotten hold of someone's felt-tip high-lighter. Now the little boy's hands and face were covered with smudges of bright pink ink. "I'm going to have to take you into the bath-room and wash you off. Let's get going."

She took Alex by the hand and started out of the room. "Say, Darce and Allie," she called over her shoulder. "Could you watch Nicky while I take Alex to get cleaned up?"

"Sure!" Darcy called cheerfully. "We'll take

him down to the gym with us and meet you there.''

Allie stood up. ''Come on, Nicky!'' she called.

There was no answer. Stephanie paused in the doorway. ''Nicky?'' she called. ''Come on out from wherever you're hiding.''

The room was completely silent. Stephanie turned around and came back inside. ''Where *is* Nicky, anyway?'' she asked, beginning to lose her temper. She took a few steps and peered around the corner of the biography section. ''He has to be somewhere around here. Do you know where Nicky is, Alex?''

Alex looked perplexed and shook his head no.

''He's not over here,'' Darcy called, checking behind the mystery shelf.

''Or here, either,'' Allie reported from the picture-book area.

''He's not under the table,'' said Darcy, getting down on her hands and knees.

''Or behind the door, or Mr. Mason's desk,'' said Allie.

''He's not over here by the fish tank,'' said Darcy.

"But where can he have gone?" Stephanie asked. She was beginning to feel anxious. Quickly she ran around the library checking and rechecking all the places everyone had already looked. As she looked, her stomach slowly tied itself into a big, painful knot. By the time she'd finished poking into every single corner, she was really worried.

Allie took one more look into Mr. Mason's supply closet. Then she crossed the room and said softly, "I don't think he's in here anymore, Steph."

"Me either," Darcy agreed from the opposite corner.

Stephanie looked at her friends and blinked back sudden tears.

They're right, she told herself. *It's time to face the facts. Nicky is gone. And it's all my fault!*

CHAPTER

7

◆ ◀ ◢ ◆

"The important thing," Stephanie said, "is not to panic." She wrung her hands together and bit her lip. "WHERE IN THE WORLD IS HE?" she screamed at the top of her lungs. "WE HAVE TO FIND HIM. *NOW!*"

Allie hurried over and patted her on the shoulder. "Calm down, Steph," she said soothingly. "After all, Nicky's only two years old. How far can he have gotten?"

Stephanie thought of some of the places the twins had gotten into at home. "You'd be amazed," she said.

"Well, he can't have been gone very long, or one of us would have noticed," Allie said.

Stephanie swallowed hard. She realized she hadn't paid the slightest bit of attention to the twins for over half an hour. *If I—the boys' own cousin and baby-sitter—wasn't watching them, how could I have expected anyone else to keep track of them?* she thought frantically.

"All we have to do," Allie was saying, "is go get the other kids out of the gym, get organized, and spread out through the school. That way we can make a thorough search for him."

Stephanie worked hard to pull herself together. "Okay," she said. "Let's get going." She hoisted Alex up onto her hip. "You're staying with me!" she told him. "I'm not taking a chance on you getting lost like Nicky."

"Lost," Alex repeated cheerfully. "Nicky lost."

The three girls went out into the hall. "Allie and I will go get the other kids," Darcy said, starting off toward the gym. "Half of us will cover the cafeteria and the auditorium. The other half will do the teachers' lounge and the locker rooms. You and Alex can check out everything else, Steph."

"But what about all the classrooms?" Stephanie said. She had a sudden, awful thought and had to fight back a flood of tears. "What about the doors to the outside?" she wailed. "What if Nicky got out of the building?"

Darcy looked at her friend in dismay. "We'd better get going," she said quickly. "Fast." She and Allie hurried off down the hall.

With Alex happily yanking at her long hair, Stephanie went off in the other direction. The two of them stopped at every single classroom they passed. Fortunately, some of the rooms were locked and didn't have to be searched. But some rooms had been left open for the cleaning staff.

Stephanie insisted on going into each and every possible place. With Alex under her arm, she checked under all the teachers' desks and behind every map rack or art table. She even looked in places where she knew Nicky couldn't possibly fit, like inside overflowing supply cabinets or behind bookshelves.

"Nicky!" she called as she looked. "Nicky! If you're hiding, you'd better come out right now! Can you hear me?"

But Nicky's little voice didn't answer. Finally, after a long, frantic search, only a few more places remained to be checked. As she approached the auditorium, Stephanie was almost beside herself with panic and guilt.

"How could I have done this?" she asked herself. "I *knew* it was wrong to bring the twins here to my school—especially without telling anyone. And then, after I brought them here, I couldn't even be bothered to watch them." Stephanie didn't realize she was talking out loud as she berated herself. "For all I know, Nicky could have wandered away a long time ago. He could be anywhere by now!"

The image of Becky's worried face came into her mind, and Stephanie's stomach twisted tighter. "How could I have done this?" she asked herself again. "What will I tell Becky if Nicky's been hurt—or maybe even lost forever? She'll never forgive me. I'll never forgive *myself*."

As she walked toward the auditorium, she ran into Darcy and her search party. "Any sign of him?" she asked them hopefully.

"No," Darcy said. She pointed at the auditorium. "But I'll bet he's in here for sure. He's probably hiding under the seats."

"I hope so," Stephanie said shakily. She

shifted Alex, who was beginning to feel like he weighed a ton, to her other hip. Then she hurried into the auditorium.

"Nicky!" she called, peering under a row of seats. "Come out here right now! Please?"

Her own voice bounced off the walls and echoed in her ears. But there was no answer from Nicky. At that moment, Stephanie was filled with despair. All she wanted to do was sit down in the middle of the floor and burst into tears.

"I think we're going to have to call the police," she told Darcy in a quavering voice.

"Yo, Stephanie!" Christopher Ripple's voice rang through the empty auditorium. "Come out here!"

Stephanie whirled around and raced out into the hall. Chris was standing in the doorway of a room labeled BOYS. "Come stick your head in here for a minute, Stephanie," he said. "I think you'll like what you see."

For the first time in her life, Stephanie looked into the boys' room at John Muir Middle School. What she saw there made her grin from ear to ear. Nicky was standing in front of one of the toilets. He was happily tossing sheet after sheet of toilet paper into the water. From the looks of the toilet, he'd been doing this for a long time.

Stephanie was so happy to see him, she couldn't say a word. She handed Alex to Chris. Then she ran into the boys' room, grabbed Nicky, and squeezed him as hard as she could. Over her shoulder, Nicky threw one last sheet of paper into the toilet.

Then the floodgates burst, and Stephanie really did start crying. "Oh, Nicky," she sobbed into his fluffy baby hair. "I thought I'd lost you! I thought I was never going to find you again! Oh, Nicky. I'm so glad to see you."

"Cwying," Nicky said, with a serious expression on his face. "Stephanie cwying."

"Excuse me." In the doorway, Chris cleared his throat. "Um, Stephanie? Don't you think we should go back and tell everyone else we found Nicky? And, well, it is getting pretty late. Are we going to work on the carnival any more this afternoon?"

Stephanie stood up. She yanked a sheet of toilet paper from the roll on the wall and used it to dry her eyes.

"You guys are going to have to manage without me for the rest of the afternoon," she told Chris. "Go ahead and get as much made as you can. But I have to get these boys back home. Fast."

She scooped Nicky up under one arm. Then she reached out and took Alex under the other. As she followed Chris back to the library, she realized that her legs were trembling as she walked.

"Never again," she whispered to Nicky and Alex. "I'm never going to do something so stupid again in my entire life."

She hurried into the library, where she hastily put on the boys' hats and jackets. Then she stuffed the twins into their stroller and ran out the door. As she jogged through the streets toward her house, she was shaking. *Something really terrible could have happened,* she thought again and again. And if it had, she would have had no one to blame but herself. She had been both careless and irresponsible.

Breathless, Stephanie turned onto her own block and started pushing the stroller along the sidewalk. "There's only one good thing about this," she said as she puffed up the hill. "And that is that Nicky *didn't* get hurt. He's safe. And so is Alex. At least I was lucky about that."

She took the boys out of the stroller and carried them up the steps to the house. "In some ways," she said as she opened the door, "this was actually a very lucky afternoon."

She smiled as she stepped into the living room. But then she caught her breath in dismay. The scene she saw made her realize something right away. Without a doubt, her "lucky" afternoon had just come to a very abrupt end.

CHAPTER
8

♦ ◀ ♦ ♦

Becky and Jesse sat side-by-side on the living-room couch. Becky was holding a box of tissues on her lap. Her eyes were red and puffy, and Stephanie could tell she had been crying.

Jesse didn't look very happy either. His face was drawn and worried. In his right hand, he clutched the telephone as if his life depended on it.

When she saw Stephanie walk through the door with the twins, Becky let out a little scream. "Nicky! Alex!" she cried, jumping to her feet. "You're all right. Oh, thank goodness. I was so worried."

As Becky talked, she started crying all over again. She ran across the room and grabbed the twins up in her arms. "Oh, Stephanie," she said. "What happened? Where have you been?"

Stephanie swallowed hard. "Uh . . ." she said. She looked at the clock on the wall. "You're not supposed to be here for at least three minutes, Becky. What are you doing home already? What happened to your class?"

"The instructor got sick," Becky said. "So they canceled it." She picked up the boys and carried them over to the couch. She sat down and snuggled them on her lap.

Stephanie's heart sank. Becky's class had been canceled! She'd never even thought about that happening.

"When I got home," Becky went on, in between hugging and kissing her sons, "and saw you weren't here, I decided you must have gone back to the playground the way you did last week. So I thought it would be fun to surprise you all and meet you. But when I got there, *you* weren't there."

"She already knows that, Becky," Jesse said grimly.

"So then," Becky said, "I came back here again. I checked the backyard. Then I searched the whole house over. And then I began to panic. I *knew* you never would have taken the boys off somewhere without leaving a note. Or unless something was wrong. So I got really upset."

"With good reason," Jesse said. "Becky was *so* upset, she called me. She had a hard time tracking me down, because I was in the middle of a big recording session with the band. But once she got me, I came right home. We've been sitting here for half an hour, calling everyone we could think of who might possibly know where you've been."

Becky stopped kissing the twins and looked up. "So where *have* you been, Stephanie?" she asked.

Slowly, Stephanie pulled off her jacket and came the rest of the way into the room. "Uh, well," she said. "You remember those committee meetings at my school I told you about, Becky? I had to go to one of them. So, well, I took the boys with me."

Becky stared at her. "You *what?*"

"Well, see, I'm the chairperson of the committee, and my classmates weren't getting along very well without me, so I thought you wouldn't mind if I just popped the twins into their stroller and—"

"You walked through all those busy city streets to your school with my babies!" Becky said. She handed the boys to Jesse and got to her feet. "Without getting permission from either one of us?"

Stephanie cringed. She had never seen Becky look so furious. And her voice was as cold and hard as an ice cube.

"Well, I didn't think you'd mind. . . ." Stephanie began. Her voice trailed off as she tried to meet Becky's eyes and found that she couldn't.

"The very fact that you didn't tell me where you were going shows that you knew very well I *would* mind, Stephanie Tanner!"

"But nothing bad happened to them, Aunt Becky," Stephanie said. She thought of how she'd managed to lose Nicky, and her cheeks flamed. *How did I get into the habit of lying all the time?* she asked herself. "There was really nothing to worry about."

"Well, we *were* worried," Becky said angrily. "Very worried."

Jesse got to his feet. "I can't believe I'm hearing this!" he said angrily. "You are standing there, making excuses for something that you absolutely knew was wrong, Stephanie! You had no permission to take the boys so far away. You certainly should have asked someone before you did something like that. And the reason you didn't ask was that you knew what the answer would have been: N-O. NO! *And—*"

"*And,*" Becky interrupted, "I'm beginning to suspect that you took the boys to your school last week when you said you had them at the playground!"

"Well," Stephanie said, "I never actually said I'd had the boys at the playground—"

"Stephanie!" Becky's voice cut like a sharp steel knife. "In my book, not 'actually' telling the truth is the exact same thing as telling a lie." She reached out and took Alex back from Jesse. "I cannot believe I thought you were responsible enough to be in charge of our children. You clearly have a lot to learn about the meaning of the word trust."

Becky and Jesse started up the stairs with the boys. "But until you do learn how to be responsible, Stephanie," Jesse added, "we are firing you as our baby-sitter. Starting now."

When her aunt and uncle were gone, Stephanie stood in the middle of the living room for a long, agonizing moment. She had never felt so ashamed of herself. And, she realized, she still hadn't told them the whole truth. She hadn't mentioned to Becky and Jesse that she hadn't even been watching the boys and that she'd actually managed to lose one of them. If they knew that, she told herself, they'd probably never even speak to her again. But at least then she would have been completely honest.

For a few seconds, she thought about following them up to the attic, coming clean about what had really happened at school, and apologizing. But after a while, she realized she just couldn't make herself do it. She'd already disappointed Becky and Jesse so much. She couldn't imagine what they would say or do if they knew the whole, horrible story. It was just too terrible to think about.

She hung up her jacket and straggled up the stairs to her room. There she flopped down on her bed and stared up at the ceiling.

"You've really done it this time, Stephanie," she said out loud. Then, for the second time that day, she started to cry.

She didn't hear a thing when Comet nosed open her door and trotted into the room. But when the dog leaped onto her bed and slobbered on her wet cheek, she turned gratefully toward him. "Thanks, Comet," she whispered. "It's nice to know somebody around here still likes me enough to lick my face."

She was still lying on her bed an hour later when D.J. knocked on the door.

"Are you okay, Steph?" her sister asked.

"I guess so." Stephanie rolled over on her side. "Did Becky tell you what happened?"

"Jesse did," D.J. said. "He's still very angry about it. And I have to confess I was pretty surprised to hear you'd do something like that."

"Don't *you* start in on me!" Stephanie interrupted. "I've already had lectures from Jesse and Becky! You should have heard them.

D.J., they were positively screaming at me."

"Well, for all they knew, you and the boys might have been kidnapped!"

"I know." Stephanie groaned. She rolled over and put her face down on her bed. "Believe me, I know." She made a fist and punched her pillow. "How could I have done something so stupid?"

"I don't know, Steph," her father's voice answered. "That's exactly what I keep asking myself."

Stephanie sat up in surprise. "When did you get home?" she asked him.

"A few minutes ago," Danny answered. "As soon as I walked in the door, Joey filled me in."

"*Joey* told you? Oh, great. Now everybody knows I messed up. It'll probably be on TV tonight. Sixth-grader Stephanie Tanner Takes Twins to School Without Permission. Film at Eleven."

Danny came over and sat on the edge of her bed. "We all know it's difficult to keep secrets in a house like this," he said quietly.

"Difficult?" Stephanie repeated. "It's impossible, Dad. Everybody knows everybody's business. It's just not fair! It's positively—"

"Stephanie," Danny broke in. "You and I both know you're complaining about privacy right now because you don't want to talk about the real issue, which is your behavior. And anyway, your behavior *is* my business, because I'm your father."

"Oh."

Danny ran a hand through his dark hair. "To think I was so proud of you I was actually bragging about how you were old enough and mature enough to be a responsible baby-sitter. What made you do this, Stephanie?"

A fresh set of tears started down Stephanie's cheeks. "It was the committee at school, Dad," she said. "It's important to me, and the kids really needed my help."

"But hadn't you already agreed to baby-sit for Becky on Tuesday afternoons?"

"Yes," Stephanie said. "And that's why I took the twins with me. It was because I didn't want to let Becky down!"

"But you *did* let Becky down by scaring her half to death. You also let down Jesse by scaring him, and by making him leave his recording session, which had to be rescheduled. Did you know he's going to have to pay for this afternoon's studio time anyway, even though he didn't get anything out of it?"

Danny got to his feet. "You let down Alex and Nicky," he went on, "by taking them all the way to your school without permission. And you let me down too, for that matter, as well as the rest of the family."

He started out of the room. "I want you to think about that long and hard, Stephanie. Because it's very, *very* important that you understand it."

As soon as the door closed after Danny and D.J., Stephanie started crying all over again. "I *do* understand it, Dad," she said out loud. "I understand it better than you—because I'm the only one who knows the whole, terrible story. I'm the only one who knows just how many people I've let down. Why? Because in addition to my family, tomorrow I'm going to have to go to school and let all my friends down. Why? Because after what I did today, there's absolutely no way I can ever ask Uncle

Jesse to bring his band to the carnival. And the sixth-grade project is going to be the absolute, total *pits!*"

She rolled over and punched her pillow one more time. "I've really done it this time," she went on. "This time I've gotten myself into something I just can't get out of. And I've totally ruined my entire life!"

CHAPTER
9

♦ ◄ ◆ ♦

The next morning, Stephanie got up and put on her brightest, most springlike outfit—a yellow-and-pink flowered T-shirt and yellow miniskirt. *Maybe if I* look *cheerful*, she told herself, *everybody will* act *cheerful when they see me.*

In this hopeful mood, she bounced down the stairs to the kitchen. "Good morning, everyone," she said.

Jesse glanced at her over the rim of his coffee-cup and scowled.

Everyone else just mumbled and continued with his or her breakfast. In fact, Alex was the only one who really seemed to get excited about Stephanie's entrance. When she passed his high chair, he reached out one of his chubby hands and smeared a huge glob of banana-rice cereal across the front of her yellow skirt.

"Alex!" she began indignantly. She stopped when she realized everyone in the family was staring at her, waiting to hear what she would say.

"I'll just wipe that right off!" she said with forced brightness. "Fortunately, banana is yellow, so it's almost a perfect match for my skirt. I just know it'll dry out by the time I get on the bus." She crossed to the sink and dabbed at the cereal with a wet paper towel. "And I don't think the smell will really bother anyone at school. After all, it's an organic substance, and . . ."

She stopped chattering when she realized no one was paying any more attention to her. With a sigh, she helped herself to a bowl of Fruit Toastee-O's, a cereal she normally hated. She crossed the room and sat down at the table. As she picked up her spoon, Comet trotted over and put his head in her lap. Touched, Stephanie started to scratch his ears. But as she realized what he was really doing, she pulled her hand away. Comet's long, pink tongue was slurping the side of her skirt. The dog was eagerly polishing off the rest of Alex's banana-rice cereal.

Her skirt still felt unpleasantly damp when she climbed down off the bus in the school parking lot an hour later. But none of her friends seemed to notice. Instead, they treated her like Stephanie the Great, Heroine and Champion of the Sixth Grade.

"Yo, Stephanie!" Josh Hillman called to her as she entered the school building. He closed his locker and trotted up to her. "I heard you really came through for us."

"Uh . . ."

"A rock band!" Josh said enthusiastically. "Where'd you ever come up with such a totally cool idea?"

"Uh . . ."

"I just knew you'd do it," he said. He smiled, and his beautiful blue eyes crinkled at the corners. "I already told Chris Ripple all the guys on the soccer team would like to help out with making some booths, or whatever. Now that we know our project is going to be such a winner." He started off down the hall. "I'll catch you later, so you can fill me in on what to tell the guys. Bye.''

''Bye,'' Stephanie said feebly.

As she watched Josh walk away, she was surprised to discover she could feel even worse than she had before. *Wonderful*, she thought. In just a few short hours, the rock band idea had spread all over the school. For now, the whole sixth grade loved her. But just wait until they heard she couldn't possibly ask Uncle Jesse to play at the carnival.

''Yoo-hoo! Stephanie!'' Kara's song carried down the hall. ''I am having so much fun telling everybody about your great idea about the rock band. And now we have lots more volunteers to help. Once the kids heard about the rock band, they were really psyched!''

''Mmmm.''

The bell rang for first period. ''Gotta run, Steph! See you later! Tootles!''

''Tootles,'' Stephanie muttered to Kara's departing back. She had started to slink off to her social studies class when someone tapped her on the shoulder.

''Guess what, Steph?'' Darcy said. ''You and

Allie and I get to go to the library again this period so we can finish up our Colonial life projects. I already have passes for the three of us!"

"Oh, good," Stephanie said. She turned around and followed her friend toward the library. At least, she thought, this meant she wouldn't have to face an entire roomful of people who still believed she was Heroine of the Sixth Grade. Not until second period, anyway.

"So give," Darcy said as soon as they sat down at their favorite table in the library.

"Give?"

"Yeah! Tell me what music your uncle said his band is going to play for everybody at the carnival."

"Wait!" Allie hurried into the room and put her books on the table. "Don't say anything without me. I want to hear all about the rock band too. Absolutely everybody who's anybody is talking about it!"

"Tell me something I don't know," Stephanie said dryly.

"So what did your uncle say?" Darcy demanded. "Is he going to play golden oldies? Or Elvis? Or new stuff? Or what?"

"W-well," Stephanie stammered. "To be honest, Uncle Jesse didn't really have much of anything to say to me last night. See, when I got home from the library, there was, like, a little family problem."

"Oh, well," Allie said. "It doesn't matter. He can play anything he wants as far as I'm concerned. He's so cool looking, everybody will go wild for him no matter what he plays."

"Right," Darcy agreed. "It must be a blast living in the same house with a real rock star, right, Steph?"

"Well, now that you mention it," Stephanie began, "it's not always all that easy. Just last night, Uncle Jesse and I—"

"Star temperament," Darcy broke in. "All those movie stars and performers have it. Lots of ups and downs. They're not *supposed* to be easy to live with!"

"I've heard that too," Allie said. "It's something to do with the creative personality. It's what makes celebrities so interesting and exciting. Isn't that right, Steph?"

"Well, I'd have to agree with the ups-and-downs part," Stephanie said. She looked at her friends' excited faces and realized there was no way she could bear to disappoint them about Uncle Jesse's band. And maybe, she thought, just maybe she'd be able to figure out a way to make the carnival work after all. Maybe she could make up with her uncle. Or maybe she could think of a different idea.

After school, as she worked with the other kids in the gym, Stephanie couldn't bring herself to tell her friends she didn't really have a rock band for the carnival—which was only three days away. Almost everyone in the sixth grade had offered to help in some way. During their study halls and lunch periods, volunteers took turns hammering boards, painting booths, preparing refreshments, sorting out prizes, and organizing work schedules. As they worked, the kids talked and joked and screamed with laughter. Everyone was having a wonderful time. Everyone, that is, except Stephanie. Though she smiled at her classmates' jokes, she didn't make any herself. She was too miserable inside to joke around for a single, solitary moment.

But bad as things were at school, things at

home were even worse. On Thursday, when Stephanie got home from school, she discovered Becky in the middle of a telephone conversation.

"Yes, that's right," her aunt was saying. "I need someone for the next three Tuesday afternoons from three-thirty to about six."

Becky was hiring a baby-sitter to replace her! Stephanie froze in the doorway. Her mouth dropped open with dismay.

"Yes," Becky went on. "For twin boys." She glanced up and met Stephanie's gaze.

Stephanie blinked and swallowed hard. "You hired someone else to baby-sit for Nicky and Alex?" she asked when Becky had hung up.

Becky looked surprised. "Yes, of course I did," she said.

Stephanie didn't know what to say. Uncle Jesse said she was fired from her baby-sitting job, but it really hadn't sunk in until now.

"I'm sorry, Stephanie. But look at it from my point of view. How could I do anything else after what happened? If I didn't find a new baby-sitter, I wouldn't be acting like a responsible parent." She stood up. "And speaking of responsible parents, I have to go upstairs and check to see if the boys are awake from their naps."

Becky hurried up the stairs. Stephanie followed more slowly. When she walked into her room, she saw that Michelle was already there. She was sitting in the middle of Stephanie's bed, reading one of Stephanie's books and wearing one of Stephanie's sweatshirts.

Stephanie was too depressed to get angry. "Move over," was all she said. Then she flopped down in her usual position on the bed.

Michelle stared at her in surprise. "Are you sick, Stephanie?" she asked.

"Yes, Michelle. I am sick. Sick of my life."

"Should we call the doctor?" her little sister asked in alarm.

"No," Stephanie said with her face in her pillow. "The kind of sick I am just means—well, I guess it just means sad."

"Oh," Michelle said sympathetically. "That's too bad. What's the matter?"

Stephanie thought of the deep, dark hole she'd dug for herself and sighed. "It's so complicated," she said. "It would take forever to explain. But I'm still sad about it. You can trust me on that."

"I know what'll cheer you up!" Michelle announced. She jumped off the bed. "Dah dah de dah de *dum*."

With a flourish, she started dancing around the room, loudly belting out a jazzed-up version of her worm song:

> *"One hundred giggling worms,*
> *Ho, ho, ho!*
> *Cha cha cha!*
> *One hundred wiggling worms,*
> *High and low!*
> *Boe dee oh!"*

Under normal circumstances, Stephanie would have thought Michelle's "cool" version of the worm song was hysterically funny. But tonight she was feeling too sorry for herself, and she hardly even noticed the changes.

When Michelle finally finished her song— after five renditions—Stephanie decided to go ask D.J. for some advice about her situation. D.J., who was still studying for her French test, didn't even glance up when Stephanie came in.

"Hi, Steph," she said over her shoulder. *"Comment allez-vous?"*

"If that means 'How are you?' then the answer is 'Terrible,' Deej."

D.J. stuck a finger in her book to mark her place. She swept her hair away from her face and looked up. "Are you still worrying about Aunt Becky and Uncle Jesse being mad at you?"

"I guess you could say that," Stephanie said.

D.J. looked sympathetic. "Well, I wish I had some advice for you," she said. "But if you've already said you're sorry, I'm not sure there's all that much more you can do—other than try to show everybody how responsible you're capable of being. And how honest. That's really important, since they need to feel like they can trust you again." She looked back down at her book. "You know what they say, Steph. Time heals all wounds. Aunt Becky and Uncle Jesse will forgive you—sooner or later."

Stephanie stared at her sister's bent head. She'd been planning to tell D.J. about the lie she'd told about the rock band. She wanted to ask D.J. for advice about what to tell her friends. But now D.J. was sitting there telling her to be honest about everything!

She'll just say I should tell the truth, Stephanie thought miserably. *And that's the last thing I want to do.*

She hadn't been honest about anything lately, she realized as she walked out of D.J.'s room. She hadn't been honest with Becky about what she'd been doing with the kids after school. She hadn't been honest about how she'd almost lost Nicky. And she hadn't been honest with the kids at school about not being able to get a rock band.

She sighed again and went to answer the phone, which had been ringing repeatedly.

"Hi, Steph!" Darcy said. "Can you go to the mall after school tomorrow? My mom says she'll drive. I need to pick up some more prizes for the fish pond at the discount store. Plus I heard there's a big sale on blue jeans."

"I guess so," Stephanie said.

"Terrific! I'll call Allie and see if she can come with us. Okay?"

"I guess so."

"Well, you don't sound very excited about it, Stephanie! You're usually the first one in line for a mall trip. Are you sick or something?"

"Yeah. I mean, no, I'm fine. And I'd love to go to the mall. I'll meet you in front of the telephone booth at school as soon as last period lets out tomorrow."

"Fab!" Darcy said. "And be sure to bring some money so we can shop till we drop. Bye!"

"Bye," Stephanie said. She hung up the phone, went into her room, and crawled right back into her bed.

That night she had terrible dreams. In one, she was standing up on a stage in front of the entire school, dressed in a pair of Michelle's Care Bear pajamas. All the kids were pointing at her and laughing and jeering. When she tried to escape, she ran right into the rest of her family, along with Comet and Kimmy Gibbler.

The dream went on. "I'm so disappointed in you, Stephanie," her father was saying.

"*Moi*, too," said D.J.

"We don't trust you," said Becky and Jesse together.

"As the cow said to the bull," said Joey, "it's time for you to moooove out, Stephanie!"

"Out you go," said Michelle. "Boe dee oh!"

"Do you have anything to eat?" said Kimmy. "I'm starving-ay voo!"

For the entire six long hours at school the next day, Stephanie kept remembering her nightmare and shuddering. By the time she was in Darcy's mother's car on the way to the mall after school, she was a wreck. While Allie and Darcy chattered on about the upcoming carnival, she huddled in the corner of the backseat, wrapped up in complete gloomy silence. She was still quiet when they arrived at the mall and made arrangements to meet Darcy's mother in two hours.

"Let's hit the food court!" Darcy suggested. "I could die for a bag of curly fries."

"I want a Fruit Slushee," said Allie. "And a bag of curly fries. What about you, Steph?"

"Me?" Stephanie answered absently. "Oh, I'm not really hungry."

Allie and Darcy exchanged puzzled glances.

"Well," Allie said, "if you change your mind, you can have some of my fries."

The three girls went into the mall and climbed onto the escalator that went up to the food court. As they reached the top, Allie suddenly grabbed Stephanie's arm. "Look at *that!*" she exclaimed, pointing her finger.

Stephanie and Darcy looked straight ahead at a giant, life-sized picture of Dara Dean. They went closer to read the words at the bottom of the poster.

"Have your picture taken with movie star Dara Dean!" Darcy read out loud. "Sponsored by the eighth grade. All proceeds go to benefit the John Muir Middle School Library Fund."

"Oh," Allie breathed as they continued toward the food court. "Can you believe it? They're not even going to bother trying to get money from the kids at school or their parents. They're planning to set up a booth right here in the mall. Just think of all the money they can make charging people to have their pictures taken with Dara Dean!"

"Jenni Morris's dad could have some kind of show biz contacts," said Darcy. "Maybe that's how they were able to get Dara Dean to agree to work for them.''

''Maybe,'' Allie said. She stopped at the curly fries booth and ordered an extra-large bag. ''But that doesn't matter to us, does it?'' she added with a smile. ''We've got show biz contacts too!''

Darcy put her arm around Stephanie's shoulders. ''Miss Stephanie Tanner,'' she said. ''Our rock star connection. The sixth grade's ticket to fame, fortune . . . and a day off from school!''

All at once, Stephanie couldn't stand it anymore. ''But that's just the problem,'' she said, collapsing onto a metal chair. ''I *don't* have a rock star connection! Not anymore! I had a big fight with Uncle Jesse and Aunt Becky, and now Uncle Jesse is hardly even speaking to me—let alone doing any favors for me.''

Allie and Darcy's mouths dropped open. ''You mean you never even asked your uncle if his band would play for the carnival?'' Allie asked in disbelief. ''You've got to be kidding!''

''Is this some kind of joke?'' Darcy asked.

Miserably, Stephanie shook her head. For a

long minute, her friends stared at her in shock. Then Darcy got to her feet.

"I'm calling the other kids on the fund-raising committee," she announced. "If they can get to the mall in the next half hour, we'll still have time for an emergency meeting. Maybe one of them will have an idea of what to do about this."

"I'll help you," Allie said, standing up and following her toward the phone booth.

While Stephanie sat silently on her chair, Darcy and Allie called all the members of the sixth-grade committee. Luckily, most of the kids were home and were able to come to the mall. By four-thirty almost the entire committee was sitting around a table in the food court.

"Stephanie," Darcy began, "has something to tell all of you."

Stephanie felt like crying. "Couldn't you tell them, Darcy?" she pleaded.

"No," Darcy said firmly. "You have to tell them. And fast. We don't have that much time."

"Okay," Stephanie said in a tiny voice. "I—I

can't ask my uncle to come to the carnival. So . . . well . . . the sixth grade doesn't have a rock band after all."

"What?" said Chris Ripple. "This is unbelievable!"

"Why did you let us put up posters all over the school saying we were going to have a rock band?" Kara asked. "Now we look like a bunch of idiots!"

"We sure do," said Lizzie Timmons. "I'm embarrassed to even be on this committee anymore." She pushed back her chair and got to her feet. "In fact, I quit. Good-bye!"

"Me too!" several other kids chimed in. "I'm outta here."

Lizzie started to walk away, but Stephanie reached out and grabbed her sleeve. "Wait, Lizzie," she said. "Wait, everybody else. Don't leave yet. Just listen to me for one minute."

Reluctantly, the committee members stopped and turned around to listen. "Look," Stephanie said, "I know I've really messed this whole thing up. And I mean big time."

"You can say that again!" said Kara.

Stephanie's cheeks flamed, but she kept going. "I know you all feel like quitting. But stop and think about all the work we've put in so far. All that planning and hammering and painting. You don't want to waste that, do you?"

Christopher and Lizzie looked at each other. "Well," Chris began, "it's true we've made a lot of stuff already."

"Right," Stephanie said. "And look at it this way. Even if our carnival doesn't win first prize—"

"Which it certainly won't!" Kara interrupted. "Without a rock band."

Stephanie ground her teeth and ignored her. "Even if our carnival doesn't win first prize," she continued, "we'll still earn at least *some* money for the library. And that's what we were supposed to be trying to do in the first place, wasn't it?"

Lizzie nodded. "Okay," she said, coming back to the table. "I vote to go ahead and have our carnival. You've convinced me, Stephanie. Which doesn't mean I'm not still really, really mad at you."

"As co-chairperson," Darcy said, "I call for a quick vote. Let's have a show of hands for all those in favor of going ahead with the carnival."

One by one, each committee member raised his or her hand. "Okay," Darcy said. "The yes votes have it. So we'll go on with the show as planned. And hope for the best."

And hope for the best, Stephanie repeated to herself. *Because I don't think things can possibly get much worse.*

CHAPTER
10

◆ ◀ ◆ ◆

The Saturday of the carnival was sunny and clear. Bright and early at seven-thirty, all the sixth-grade volunteers arrived at the school, ready to work. They spent the rest of the morning busily setting up booths and other activities. To their surprise, a full half hour before the auction was scheduled to be held in the gym, parents and children had already started lining up at the carnival entrance.

"Baby-sitting during the auction!" one delighted father exclaimed. "What a great idea. We didn't know how we were going to manage Toni and Paolo while the bidding was going on!"

"Business is looking good," Allie whispered to Stephanie as they frantically sold admission tickets. "Maybe we'll win that day off after all."

"I wouldn't count on that," Stephanie whispered back. "But at least we'll have given it the old John Muir Middle School try!"

By one-thirty, almost all the parents had gone inside for the auction and the carnival grounds were overflowing with little kids. At first, the sixth graders were thrilled to have so many customers. The little boys and girls seemed to love all the activities, such as the obstacle course, the cakewalk, and the arts and crafts tables.

"We're going to make a fortune!" Darcy called to Stephanie from the fish pond. "Uh-oh! Wait a minute, Suzy. Put down that box of prizes! Come back here!"

"*Wah!*" yelled a little boy. "I didn't win a cake!"

A little girl dropped her cookie. "I want my mommy!" she screamed.

Before long, similar shouts and cries were echoing throughout the playground. Within only minutes, it seemed as if crazed little kids were everywhere—running and falling, hitting and crying, chasing and being chased. Some booths wobbled and fell over. An entire table full of lemon poppyseed cakes crashed to the ground. Kara Landford went into hysterics.

All over the playground, wild-eyed sixth graders darted to and fro, feebly trying to keep order. "Come back here, you!" they yelled. "Stop kicking me! Don't pull my hair, either, you little monster!"

As Stephanie watched the chaos, she became more and more horrified. "I've got to do something about this," she finally said, "or the parents are going to march out here and demand their money back. Darcy! Allie! Come here! Fast!"

With her friends' help, she finally managed to round up all the little kids together in the obstacle course area. "Okay, guys," she said, jumping up on a wooden platform. "It's time to stop running around like a bunch of maniacs, because now we're going to do something really fun. Umm . . . we're going to—"

"*WAH!*" cried a little girl. "Daddy! Daddy!"

"Ow!" screamed a toddler. "She bit me!"

A few kids at the front of the group got up and started racing around in circles. "Stephanie!'' Darcy hissed. "You're losing control again. Do something quick!''

"Okay!'' Stephanie said. "Now we're going to . . .'' Suddenly an idea came to her. "I know! Now we're going to sing a great song about worms! It goes like this:

> *"One hundred giggling worms,*
> *Ho, ho, ho!*
> *One hundred wiggling worms,*
> *High and low!''*

As she sang, she jumped down off the box and started making the same wiggling motions Michelle always made when she sang the song at home. To her surprise, she realized some of the kids were singing right along with her. They already knew the song!

With a big smile, Stephanie finished the song and started all over again. A few little kids ran up and formed a line behind her. After that everybody joined in.

> *"Oh, these wiggling, giggling worms,*
> *Watch them go!''*

A long, wiggling, giggling line of laughing children snaked its way in and out around the playground. Every time they finished one verse of the worm song, Stephanie would shout "One more time!" and the kids would burst into song once again.

It's amazing, Stephanie thought as she sang and danced. *This really isn't a bad little song at all. I wonder why it's so unappreciated.*

"Ho, ho, ho!"

"Hi, Stephanie."

Stephanie turned her head and was astonished to see Jesse, Becky, Alex, Nicky, Michelle, D.J., Danny, and Joey all grinning at her from behind the fish-pond screen. Her entire family had come to see the carnival!

"They're singing my song!" Michelle shouted joyfully. She ran out from behind the screen and scurried to grab onto the tail end of the line.

In between choruses of "Ho, ho, ho!" as Stephanie kept on singing, she noticed that Jesse was busily tuning up the guitar he'd been carrying. "I'm on my way to rehearsal," he explained. He glanced at his watch. "But since I'm a little early . . . do you mind if I join in?"

"Go right ahead!" Stephanie laughed. "You already know the song."

Jesse smiled back at her and jumped up onto the wooden platform. *Twang!* He loudly strummed his guitar and shouted, "Come on, dudes and dudettes! Let's get rockin' with the worm man. From the top now! One and a two and a three. One hundred giggling worms. Ho, ho, ho! Let me hear ya! One hundred wiggling worms! High and low! Yeah, baby!"

Everybody laughed and started singing the song all over again, clapping along to the beat of the guitar. As she sang, Stephanie just couldn't stop smiling. She thought she'd never heard such a beautiful sound in her life.

"Yo, Steph," Allie said into her ear. "It looks like we got a real rock star after all!"

"You're right!" Stephanie laughed. "The worm man!"

Later, when the auction and carnival were both over and all the parents and children had gone home, Stephanie, Darcy, and Allie sat on the front steps of the school, counting up the money in the various ticket boxes.

"I have ninety-five in here," Stephanie said.

"I have a hundred and five," Darcy said.

"Well, I have a hundred even," Allie said. "According to my calculations, we made three hundred dollars!"

"Wow!" said Stephanie. "That's way more than I ever thought we'd make—especially with all the problems we've had. Uh, make that all the problems *I've* had."

"I think it's fantastic," Darcy said. "It's just too bad we'll never beat the eighth graders. I mean, having your picture taken with Dara Dean—what a great idea. Does anybody else want to run over to the mall and see if their photo booth is still open? Maybe we can get *our* pictures taken with Dara." She flinched as Allie and Stephanie glared at her. "Just kidding!"

"You'd better be." Stephanie grinned. "But I do have to agree with you—a photo booth with Dara Dean is a great idea. With a fund-raiser like that, the eighth graders are probably going to top a thousand dollars today—minimum!"

CHAPTER
11

♦ ◄ ✦ ♦

Later that evening, the extended Tanner family gathered around the kitchen table for a dinner of Joey's homemade spaghetti and garlic bread. Stephanie was exhausted but very happy. She was partly happy that the carnival had been a success. But she was most happy about being back on good terms with everybody she cared about.

"I just couldn't believe my eyes, Stephanie," Becky said. "When we walked up to the playground and there you were, leading all those laughing, wiggling children in that silly song."

"Hey!" Michelle broke in. "The worm song is *not* silly!"

127

"Sorry, Michelle," Becky said with a smile. "But what I'm trying to say is this: After what I saw today, I think Stephanie really has the ability to be a good baby-sitter after all. I want to hire her back."

Suddenly Stephanie burst into tears, jumped up, and ran out of the kitchen. She dashed up the stairs to her room and threw herself face-down on her bed. Seconds later, Becky hurried in after her. "Stephanie? What is it? What did I say?"

"You said I was a good baby-sitter!" Stephanie sobbed.

"I'm sorry," Becky said. "I meant it as a compliment. Do you want me to say you're a terrible baby-sitter?"

"Yes!" Stephanie wailed. "Because at least that would be the truth." She sat up and turned her tear-streaked face toward Becky. "I was scared to tell you this before. But that second time I took the twins to my school, Nicky wandered off. I couldn't find him for more than *half an hour!* Becky, he could have been lost forever!"

Becky blinked. "Oh, gosh," she said. "I can't

believe he was lost for so long, Steph. You should have told me."

"I know," Stephanie said. "But it scared me half to death. That's why I couldn't make myself tell you about it. You and Uncle Jesse were already so mad at me, I thought you'd hate me forever!"

She started crying all over again. She would have flopped back down on her face, but Becky caught her before she could. "Come on, Stephanie," she said, giving her a big hug. "You know Jesse and I could never hate you." She pulled out a tissue and dried Stephanie's face. "We love you. And, though it's upsetting, I think your whole experience with Nicky was probably all for the good."

"You do?"

"Well, yes, because look what you've learned from it. For one thing, after a bad scare like that, you've probably realized how important it is to watch the twins every single minute."

"That's for sure!" Stephanie exclaimed. "You can't let those little guys out of your sight for two seconds or they get into something."

"Tell me about it!" Becky laughed.

Stephanie laughed too. But then she grew serious again. "I learned a lot of other things from all this too," she said. "I learned that I can get myself into a lot of trouble when I tell lies. And I learned that telling half the truth isn't the same thing as being honest. Even if the truth isn't always what you want it to be, it's better than sneaking around and trying to fool people all the time."

"I couldn't have said it better, Steph," Becky said. She patted Stephanie on the shoulder. "So anyway, now that you know how closely the twins have to be supervised, would you like to come back to work for me?"

"You want to rehire me?"

"Definitely," Becky replied. "Starting next Tuesday afternoon."

"Fantastic," Stephanie said as she returned Becky's hug. "I promise I'll never let you down again."

"Stephanie!" D.J.'s voice rang through the house. "If you want a ride to the mall, you'd better come quick. Steve and I are leaving now."

"I'm supposed to be meeting Darcy and Allie

for ice cream there," Stephanie told Becky. "We're trying to find out which class won the contest."

"See you later, Steph," Becky said. "Good luck."

Fifteen minutes later Stephanie and her two best friends were sitting at their favorite table at the food court.

"I called everyone I know," Darcy said, licking cookie-dough ice cream off a spoon. "But I just couldn't seem to find out how much money the eighth graders made with their photo booth."

"Don't look now," Allie whispered from behind her chocolate milk shake. "But here comes Jenni Morris."

Stephanie turned around and saw Jenni walking across the food court in their direction. "Hello, my little friends," she called to them. "I guess you're all probably dying to know how much money my fantastic photo project made for the eighth grade."

"Well, we were wondering," Stephanie admitted.

"We made three hundred and twenty-five

dollars!" Jenni said. "Which definitely puts us in first place."

"Three hundred and twenty-five dollars?" Darcy repeated. "That's only twenty-five dollars more than we made!"

Stephanie stared at Jenni. "That's *all* you made? With Dara Dean working for you? In person?"

Jenni brushed a lock of hair off her forehead. "Oh, that," she said. "That was just our little advertising trick to get people interested. We didn't really have Dara Dean. We just had a really cool life-size picture of her. A lot of people paid to pose with it."

Stephanie's mouth dropped open. "You're kidding!" she exclaimed. "You got people all the way over to the mall just to have their pictures taken with another picture? How could you fool people like that?"

"Well, it worked," Jenni said. "We won the contest."

"But it wasn't honest," Stephanie said. "I'll bet some people were really mad when they found out Dara Dean wasn't here in person."

Jenni's face turned a little red. "Oh, well, I

guess a few people were a little ticked off," she said casually. "No big deal." She glanced down at her huge plastic watch. "Gotta run now, kiddies. Hope you're not too disappointed about not getting that day off from school."

Allie, Darcy, and Stephanie watched Jenni walk away. "Can you believe her?" Darcy asked. "Can you believe they did that to people?"

"Yes," Stephanie said. "When it comes to Jenni, I'll believe anything!"

"I can't believe myself!" Allie exclaimed. "I forgot to tell you guys the most important thing I found out. My mom ran into Mr. Mason at the supermarket after the carnival. He said the faculty was so impressed with the kids' hard work, they were planning to award second and third prizes to the classes that didn't win."

"Wow!" Darcy said. "So what's the second prize?"

"A pizza party," Allie said.

"Fantastic," Stephanie said. She reached into her pocket and pulled out a piece of paper and a pencil.

"What's that for?" Darcy asked.

"For taking notes," Stephanie explained. "I think we should start planning next year's project right now. That way we'll have plenty of time to get ready."

Darcy and Allie both groaned. Stephanie ignored them. "I have lots of great ideas," she said, picking up her pencil. "So let's get started!"